WHATEVER NORMAL IS

Whatever
NORMAL
IS

JANE ST. ANTHONY

University of Minnesota Press
Minneapolis • London

Published by the University of Minnesota Press
111 Third Avenue South, Suite 290
Minneapolis, MN 55401-2520
http://www.upress.umn.edu

Printed in the United States of America on acid-free paper

The University of Minnesota is an equal-opportunity educator and
employer.

24 23 22 21 20 19   10 9 8 7 6 5 4 3 2 1

Library of Congress Cataloging-in-Publication Data
St. Anthony, Jane, author.
Whatever normal is / Jane St. Anthony.
Minneapolis : University of Minnesota Press, [2019] | Summary: In 1960s
    Minneapolis, seventeen-year-old Margaret and her best friends Grace and
    Isabelle contemplate whether having a job, car, and boyfriend are as fulfilling
    as they appear to be.
Identifiers: LCCN 2018024167 (print) | ISBN 978-1-5179-0677-1 (hc/j)
Subjects: | CYAC: Best friends—Fiction. | Friendship—Fiction. | Interpersonal
    relations—Fiction. | Minnesota—History—20th century—Fiction.
Classification: LCC PZ7.S1413 Wh 2015 (print) | DDC [Fic]—dc23
LC record available at https://lccn.loc.gov/2018024167

For Curt DiCamillo and Kate DiCamillo

1

Margaret reclined on the hill of thirteen bumps. A long time ago she had believed that a witch lived here, in the park, in the foreboding house behind her with the gabled windows. Two neighborhood boys, Sherman and Roger, once peeked in a basement window and saw the witch as Margaret waited, trembling behind the thick trunk of an elm. Still, with all its mysteries, childhood had been an easier place than the present.

To the north stood the water fountain where first-grade classmate Tommy Brindle had seen her fall as she rode in circles to impress him. In front of her were the thirteen bumps that her neighbor Sherman had once biked down in the dark, leaving Margaret to believe he was dead at the bottom. Lakewood Cemetery in south Minneapolis loomed in the distance, reminding her of a long and uncertain eternity.

In three years of high school, she had not found her footing. Confident girls with aspirations overwhelmed her.

She was seventeen years old and dreamed of singing and dancing on Broadway, but she had never taken a dance class or sung where anyone could hear her.

She was an inch taller than Twiggy but weighed twenty-one pounds more than the world's most famous model. Her hair was a shiny brown with reddish highlights, but in order to emulate Cher, she had to iron it regularly.

She wanted to be madly in love but hadn't been since she was thirteen—except for Paul McCartney.

She wanted to be beautiful without effort.

She wanted a future in which she wouldn't be a housewife.

When she considered it all, she felt as if she were falling down an elevator shaft.

Then she thought of the very best things she did have: her friends, Grace and Isabelle; the summer ahead; and this park, which demanded nothing.

"It's a tramp," someone said.

Margaret stirred, recognizing the voice but not knowing where she was.

"Let's get the park police." It was a lower voice. "Maybe someone can identify the body."

That voice made Margaret want to keep her eyes closed. A clump of damp grass fell on her cheek.

"At least someone can identify the uniform," Isabelle said.

"Ugly, isn't it?" said Margaret's fourteen-year-old brother, Mark.

Margaret opened one eye and looked at Isabelle. They had walked home from school together.

"Your mom wondered where you were," said Isabelle, who lived across the street from Margaret. "I thought you might be here."

"Why would you think that?"

"Because when I turned around to wave, you were crossing Thirty-Eighth Street instead of going down your alley."

"Why would you turn around?"

"I always do. It's a little habit."

"I would never have tried to find you, but Mom made me," said Mark.

"It's peaceful here," said Margaret, ignoring her brother as she looked at Isabelle. "I needed to be alone." She waited for Mark to say something like, "That must have been a relief for everyone else in the world." But he didn't say anything, which was slightly unnerving.

"Well, the park isn't going anywhere," said Isabelle as she picked up Margaret's textbooks. "You can come back another day. Let's eat at my house. I asked your mom. Maybe Grace can come, too. After all, it's Friday."

Mark struck an invisible ball with an invisible bat.

"It went over the witch's house," he said, looking

up the hill. "And there's a real witch coming down the path."

Margaret and Isabelle turned to see Grace coming down the path, her auburn hair shining in the sunshine.

"Here I am to save the day," she called.

"No, Freckles," Mark said. "You're here to make trouble."

That evening Margaret, Grace, and Isabelle climbed through Isabelle's bedroom window onto the flat porch roof of the duplex where Isabelle lived with her mother.

"We're high school juniors," Grace said. "And we're not living life to the fullest."

"We know this, Grace," said Margaret.

"We're trying." Isabelle stood up. "Anybody else want a blanket? I feel like I'm sitting on a frozen lake."

"Trying isn't enough," Grace said. "I could use a blanket, too."

"So could I," said Margaret, as Isabelle disappeared through the window. "Do you have a plan that guarantees bliss?"

"Maybe. Let's wait for Isabelle."

"How were things at Hoodlum High today?" Margaret asked.

"A lot more lively than your nun-run school.

There was a food fight that required staff intervention. As in, the principal."

Isabelle returned with blankets.

"Isabelle," said Grace. "Margaret wants a plan for success in high school."

"Isn't it a little late? We're all going to graduate next year. Besides, it's not so bad."

"It could be better," Grace said. "We each need three things. A job. A car. A boyfriend. I don't care about the order."

"We all babysit, " Isabelle said, adjusting a blanket around her shoulders.

"No, no, no," said Grace. "We need jobs in the larger world where we'll be seen for our abilities and be paid accordingly."

"We have so much homework that I can't imagine working after school," Margaret said. "You know my mom expects me to do things around the house on the weekend. Besides, Grace, you're responsible for your family. The kids will die of scurvy if you aren't in charge."

"Don't remind me. Besides, I'll be free in a few centuries if my mom doesn't have any more babies. No matter what, we need to look out for ourselves." Grace pulled the blanket over her head and arranged it so that only her eyes showed. "We babysit. We do homework. We commiserate. I run a household. Other people our age make a lot of money. They drive and have fun and don't sit on the swings on Sunday afternoons trying to figure out when their lives will begin."

Margaret's twin sisters, Karen and Kathleen, played hopscotch on the sidewalk across the street.

"You can play, too," Karen called to the girls.

"Maybe next time," said Grace.

"You say that every time," Karen said.

"Grace, you're going out with Ronnie Blake," said Isabelle. "So your situation is different."

"We're just *friends*," Grace said. "He's not my *boy*-friend. If we want to be happy, really happy, we need those three things—not pale versions of them. Do I have to repeat the three goals?"

"Maybe we could each work on getting just one of those things," Isabelle said.

"No. It's a package."

"Grace, you're crazy," said Margaret. "If it were so easy, we'd be at Murph's Turf—that drive-in we can't drive to—right now in our cars with our boyfriends after work."

"Monday," Grace said. "I'll apply for a job on Monday, and then you can apply there."

Margaret sighed with drama. "And where will that be, where it's so easy to get a job for you and your friends?"

"Downtown. I can see it now. I'll be a hostess at a restaurant where I make three dollars an hour to greet customers with a smile, smile as I seat them, and smile as I hand out menus. You two will be dishwashers."

"Let's go inside and make fudge," Isabelle said. "I'm cold.

"You have peanut butter, right?" said Grace. "I could use some peanut butter fudge."

When Margaret stood, Karen called to her again. "Will you play with us now, Margaret? Will you play hopscotch, please?"

"Maybe tomorrow. It's getting cold."

"I'm glad I'm not in third grade," Grace said, glancing across the street at the twins. "They're even more stuck than we are."

"I loved third grade, Grace," said Margaret. "Recess twice a day. Spelling bees and learning to write a business letter and perfect our penmanship. You loved it, too."

"I always knew there was more to life than cursive," Grace said. "Remember, follow my plan and all will be well."

Margaret and Isabelle looked at each other and rolled their eyes.

"Even eyeball rollers have a chance to succeed in life," said Grace, the first to crawl through the open window into Isabelle's room. "Here we go."

2

On Saturday morning, Margaret maneuvered the vacuum into corners with care, avoiding contact with the woodwork as she encouraged dirt to respond to the suction. The hum muted the noises around her: clattering breakfast dishes, babbling twins, snide remarks from her brother. The hum allowed her to escape into her head, where she mulled over conversations, imagined the afternoon, wrote stories in her head. Vacuuming, what a job it would be: paid to free your mind while your arm was on autopilot.

Someone knocked on her shoulder. "Why are you ignoring me?" asked Mark.

"Who are you, the supervisor?"

"You keep going over the same spot. You're going to suck up the carpet."

Margaret ran the vacuum cleaner up the front of Mark's high-top.

"You'll suck up my shoelaces," he screamed. "Cut it out."

It was gratifying to see the top of his shoelace stretched taut in the roller of the vacuum cleaner.

"Next, your nose," said Margaret.

Mark jerked his foot hard, and the shoelace snapped out.

Vacuuming for pay wouldn't be a bad job. Maybe she could be a hotel maid. Then she imagined cleaning bathrooms. That could be a challenge.

Which would be the easiest of the three goals that Grace had proposed? None of them seemed attainable at the moment.

She moved into the dining room and vacuumed along the built-in buffet. Dad had stripped it and all the woodwork before he and Mom moved in, and then sanded and varnished. As a young man, he had accomplished this during daylight hours before leaving to work nights as a railroad guard. Now Mom and Dad had a small platoon to help them with senseless jobs. Once they enlisted her and Mark to strip seven layers of bedroom wallpaper while a steamer spewed hot, moist air. Her hair got so curly that she had to iron it again before leaving the house.

The phone rang—not hard to hear when standing next to it. Margaret turned the vacuum off. It was Grace.

"I got a job," she said.

"You did not."

"I did."

"But we haven't started the quest."

"I know," Grace said. "But my mom's cousin is a supervisor at the Emerald Cafe downtown, and she told my mom that they're looking for responsible teenagers. I'm starting big, pie cutter."

"Your mom won't let you go to work. You do everything at home."

"I told her that it's time for Polly to take over. I was doing everything when I was her age. And I'm only going to work on weekends."

"But we do things on weekends."

"Like what? Sit on the swings at the park? Go to the drugstore for candy? You and Isabelle can apply, too, you know."

"I have to finish vacuuming." Although Grace had been her best friend forever, she had stood up to a number of Grace's whims and instructions. "I'll think about it," she said. Did she really want a job? Wasn't babysitting enough? Would a job be a road to independence?

The phone rang as soon as Margaret hung up.

"Margaret," said Isabelle. "Should we look for a job after school on Monday?"

"Grace already has one. She's probably trying to call you right now."

"She has a job? It was that easy?"

"She's Grace. She had a tip."

"Then she'll probably have a boyfriend by this afternoon. And a driver's license and a car."

"This isn't a competition, is it? That's just Grace. I'll come over when I'm done here. Maybe Grace can come over, too."

"You know where I'll be," said Isabelle.

As Margaret pushed the vacuum cleaner into the broom closet, she thought about Grace's plan to secure the three most important things in the world, according to Grace. She, Margaret, had a boyfriend once—although she was never sure if he qualified since they never talked about it. Sherman Jensen. He was so easy to look at and usually considerate—although not the sharpest knife in the drawer, as Dad said to Mom when they didn't know that Margaret could hear them. Four times, Sherman had told her that he loved her: through the porch window, during the summer after seventh grade; on the Ferris wheel at the State Fair; on their way home from a party that Mom didn't know was mixed; and the day Sherman's family moved to central Minnesota because his grandparents had vacated their home and turned it over to Sherman's family.

She never said it back—that she loved him, but once she told him that she tucked his words into a little pocket in her heart. He seemed to like that. It was a wonderful thing that someone you weren't related to would tell you he loved you. Still, she never imagined that she would marry Sherman, because she hoped to marry a professional baseball player who liked to read. But you never knew who would be available when it was time to get married.

Now it was time to go to Isabelle's. Vacuuming was a time to ponder, and being with Isabelle and Grace was a time to toss all your thoughts up in the air and, together, try to figure out what to do with them.

3

"Why do they need a pie cutter in the morning?" Isabelle asked Grace, as the three girls sat on the swings in the park after school.

"I guess that some people eat pie for breakfast," Grace said. She had explained that she would train at the Emerald on Thursday and Friday after school so that she could work on her own on Saturday. "Saturday is the ultimate shopping day downtown. Everyone who's downtown has to eat."

"At six in the morning? At the Emerald?" said Isabelle, feigning astonishment.

Grace made her eyes roll back so that only the whites showed.

"How do you know how to cut pie so that the pieces are even?" Margaret asked.

"The pie fits on a metal plate. You lock it in. Then you pull down a circular metal form that's attached above the plate. It's set to make five cuts. Clunk. Think of it as a guillotine for pies. Finally, place each piece in a diagonal row on the counter."

"What's the pay?" Isabelle asked.

"A dollar and thirteen cents per hour."

Isabelle and Margaret looked at each other. The salary was more than twice what they earned as babysitters.

"You should come down and see me at work," said Grace.

"Just to look at you?" Margaret said. "We already know what you look like."

"Maybe you could get a job there, too."

"I don't know if I really want a job," said Isabelle. "I like babysitting."

"If we each had a job, we could probably get a car," Grace said. "We could share it."

"I don't need to drive," said Isabelle. "We walk to school."

"A lot of kids live closer to school than any of us do, and they drive to school because they can," said Grace. "Especially at your hoity-toity school. We could stop at Murph's Turf whenever we feel like it."

"But we'd just be doing that to show that we could, Grace," Margaret said.

Grace sighed. "You two aren't using your imaginations. There are places that we can't get to now."

"Like?" asked Margaret.

"Like drive-in movies."

"But we can walk to the Nile if we want to see a movie."

"Margaret, it's the principle. Most kids our age

don't have to walk miles to see a movie. We would be free. Just come downtown and see me on Saturday so that I can inspire you."

"I think the Boulevard is closer than the Nile," said Isabelle.

"But it would be closer in a car," Grace said.

"The same distance, no matter how you get there," said Margaret.

"Margaret, since when do you try to get the last word in?" said Grace. "It's unbecoming. Anyway, we're talking about *time.*"

For years the threesome had taken the bus downtown, alighted on Hennepin Avenue, and walked to Walgreen's on Nicollet for a slice of cheese or sausage pizza—which was always revolving in its glass warmer at the front of the store. It didn't cost anything to look at the clothes and purses and earrings at Dayton's, Donaldson's, J. C. Penney, or Powers. Sometimes, on a Saturday, they danced to a live band on the eighth floor of Dayton's. They ate at Bridgeman's on Hennepin, but Margaret boycotted the restaurant for a month after she found her french fries piled on a wad of gum, overlooked by a dishwasher.

But this was different, going to see Grace on display.

The Emerald Cafe would have been an intimidating structure—mirrored wall panels, chandeliers of frosted glass, art deco design, balcony—if the girls had paused to take it in. Instead they focused on the people that streamed left or right to one of the long food counters. Servers staffed each station, beginning with salad and ending with pie and coffee.

At the far end, in front of the swinging kitchen doors, Grace jumped up and down, waving a spatula. Her head looked smaller.

"She's wearing a hairnet," Isabelle said to Margaret.

They couldn't race through the line because the man in front of them insisted that the server cut a thicker slice of prime rib.

"Sir," the woman said. "All slices are the same width and weight."

"Impossible," said the man.

Although the woman knit her brows tightly, she cut another slice of the rare meat.

"Let's do that to Grace," Isabelle whispered. "Tell her that we want a bigger piece of pie than she hands us."

"I think we pull our own out under that glass shade," said Margaret. "We'll have to think of something else."

The pie counter was wide enough to hold several rows, placed diagonally in a pattern. As a customer removed a piece from the front, Grace filled in from the back: blueberry, lemon meringue, strawberry rhubarb, cherry, apple, peach, key lime, banana cream, chocolate, pecan.

Grace stood by the pie guillotine, her arm around the base, smiling as if posing for an ad. Her hair was tamed into a bun at the back of her head.

"Looking for a job, girls?" she asked. "Have a piece of prune whip while you consider a career in the cafeteria sector."

"Oh, Grace, you really did it! You have a job!" said Isabelle.

"I certainly do."

Two women walked behind Margaret and Isabelle to reach the blueberry pie.

"Do you want to see the amazing speed I need to maintain?" Grace lifted a key lime pie from a large metal table.

Using his shoulder, a young man opened the swinging door as he emerged from the kitchen with a tray of prime rib.

"Hey, Grace," he said, as he smiled at her. "Any strawberry rhubarb for me?"

"Too late. I gave it to the dishwashers."

"They don't need it. They eat everything they want off the plates." He winked at Grace as he walked by, and she winked back, and he smiled at Margaret and Isabelle, who smiled back and then turned to look at each other.

"I have never seen anyone that cute," Isabelle said. "I am speechless."

"Apparently not," said Margaret. "Is he a god?"

"Not every man who wears a butcher's hat can look that stupendous," said Grace, as she transferred more pies to the back row. "But Teddy is too old for me. He's in college and works weekends when the head meat man is off."

"College?" Isabelle said. "College? Don't be flirty with him, Grace. College is too old."

"She's not being flirty," said Margaret. "She's being Grace."

"And Grace had better get back to customer service at the counter," Grace said. "It's not only about pie. It's about building relationships."

"Grace makes everything look easy, doesn't she?" Isabelle said, as the girls sat at a table on the balcony.

"She does." Margaret forked a piece of chocolate pie. "But we know she's holding stuff in. It can't be easy to be more of a mom than her mom is."

"True." Isabelle's only sighting of Grace's mother was the day that she and Margaret returned for a pair of mittens that Margaret had left at Grace's house. Grace came to the door in an apron. "Do you want to watch me make hamburgers?" she asked. "It's Bernadette's day off. There she is."

Isabelle knew that Grace called her mother by her first name.

Bernadette lay on the couch, smoking, as she watched *American Bandstand.* "Hey, girls. How's it going?"

"Good," said Margaret. Isabelle nodded.

"These kids can really dance," said Bernadette, gesturing at the TV with a cigarette.

Before leaving, the girls watched Grace turn two pounds of ground beef into perfectly circular patties.

"Do you think that the prime rib man will ask Grace out?" asked Isabelle, as they walked into the sunshine, where melting snow mingled with a winter's worth of dog urine on the sidewalk.

"He's not really a man," Margaret said. "He's more of a pre-man. Maybe if he took his white cap off I could tell."

"It looks like he shaves. His chin was a little dark like your dad's is sometimes."

"I don't like that," said Margaret. "It reminds me of apes."

"Grace could deal with an ape."

"True. She might be fond of Teddy the ape. And why wouldn't he choose her to live in his tree and bring her the best coconuts in the forest?"

"Grace has the power, doesn't she?" Isabelle said.

"I think she can have whatever she wants if she puts her mind to it. After all, she has a job. What's next?"

4

On Sunday afternoon Margaret lay on her bed, reading. Mark had disappeared, and the twins were at the park with their best friends, Teeny and Bonnie Trumble.

"Margaret," her mother called from downstairs. "Grace is on the phone."

Margaret rose reluctantly and went downstairs to the dining room, where the phone rested on top of the buffet.

"I'm having difficulty," Grace said. "Serious difficulty."

"What is it?" Grace's difficulties came in many varieties, but most verged on the theatrical.

"It's the worst thing that has ever happened to me."

"That bad?"

"Worse."

"Do you want to come over and talk about it?"

"Call Isabelle and tell her we'll meet at her place. No snoopy kids ever show up there."

"When?"

"Right now."

Margaret crossed the street as Grace pedaled up to Isabelle's. On her knees, Miss Flora, the landlady, looked up from the small circular plot where she was turning the soil with a trowel.

"What's going to pop up there, Miss Flora?" asked Grace.

"I'll plant snapdragons here," said Miss Flora. "I want to be ready when it warms up a bit more. Do you remember why they snap?"

"Of course I do. You told us when we were kids. When you squeeze the side of the flower, the flower's 'jaw' opens. Chomp, chomp."

"They're the prettiest dragons you'll ever find."

The girls sprawled in Isabelle's living room in the duplex after greeting Isabelle's mother.

"What's up, Grace?" asked Margaret, as she sat on the couch, her legs crossed at the ankles.

"Have a brownie," Isabelle said, opening a cookie tin.

"Your mom even frosts them," said Grace. "You don't realize how good you have it."

Isabelle put the tin on the coffee table, not saying anything. Margaret wondered if Isabelle was thinking that at least Grace had a dad, which Isabelle did not.

"Let's get to the heart of my problem," said Grace, who stood up in the middle of the living room. "I, who have been asked out by numerous dodo birds at the so-called educational facility I attend, have finally found the man of my dreams."

"The dodo bird is extinct," said Margaret, turning to smooth the afghan behind her on the couch.

"You make an excellent point," Grace said. "However, I have discovered that they are not all extinct. A variation of the bird exists at my high school." She cleared her throat. "Far away from that facility, previously unknown to me, is one man worthy of my affection. He is an older man, one who combines the finest qualities of youth, yet with the maturity of a seasoned adult."

"She must mean Mr. Underwood," said Margaret to Isabelle, referring to an eloquent elderly neighbor.

"As I was saying," Grace continued, "the love of my life has made an overture. But, as always is the case with true love, I see an obstacle to his devotion."

"Pray tell, what might that be?" asked Margaret.

"Teddy asked *me* for *your* phone number," Grace said.

Margaret and Isabelle stared at Grace.

"Why does he want *my* number?" Margaret asked. "Unless he wants to talk to me to find out if you have another boyfriend or something."

"Let's just say that he never asked me for my phone number. He's seen me more than he's seen you, and he only saw you for three seconds. I guess that was long enough."

Why me instead of Grace? Margaret wondered.

Grace stared at her. Margaret saw the brown eyes and freckles and wild hair of the kindergarten, wise-cracking Grace. She had been adorable then as well as now.

Grace gave Margaret a mock frown and continued. "My deeper question is, why would he ask any of us out? He could go out with college girls. But if it's a toss between the two of us, Margaret, you won. Do you know what he calls me? 'Flip.' That's short for 'flippant.'" Grace made a popping sound with her mouth, pronouncing the two *p*'s. "He thinks I'm a jokester."

"You're so much more than that, Grace," Isabelle said, her voice rising. "You're Grace."

"But why me?" Margaret's stomach cramped. "Why not you or Isabelle?"

"It's not a carnival game, Margaret," said Grace. "He doesn't just knock over one of the three clowns with a ball."

"This is going nowhere," Margaret said. "Anyway, he won't call. It's stupid." What would she do if he did call? She couldn't talk to him when the only phone was in the dining room. Even if he asked her out, Mom and Dad would never let her go out with someone who could be nineteen or twenty.

"I gave him your number," said Grace.

"That doesn't mean that he'll call or that I'll ever go out with him."

"We'll see," Grace said. Margaret couldn't read

her, which was disturbing. "Teddy asked me where you live."

"What did you tell him?"

"I said that you lived close to me."

"You didn't."

"I did. But he doesn't know where I live."

"I don't want to hear any more about stupid Teddy," said Margaret. Her churning stomach told her that she was lying. "I promise that I would never go out with someone that you like, Grace."

"I know you wouldn't. But I'm not interested in him anymore, after what he did."

"Let's play Scrabble or watch TV or something," said Isabelle.

"Why not?" said Grace. "My life is over before it's begun. Hope has eluded me once more. There's nothing for me to do but sink into spinsterhood."

"It's silly to talk about Teddy and things that won't happen," Isabelle said.

Grace sighed. "At least the three of us have today together."

"There is no one I'd rather be with than you two," said Margaret. "No one will ever come between us. No one else is worth it." Just saying this calmed her heart as she tried to stop thinking about Teddy, which was impossible to do.

5

On the way to school, Isabelle dropped a bomb on Margaret, who was so caught up in the idea of being called by Teddy and what he might say that she was thrilled for any distraction.

"I'm getting a dog, Margaret. Actually, a puppy."

"Your mom will let you have a dog?"

"She brought it up."

"I never thought of you with a dog. Or about you and your mother stepping into poop on your sidewalk."

"One of my mom's fifth-graders has a dog who had puppies. So this boy, Harley, brought a picture of the puppies to school, and my mom said that she'd let me pick out one if I wanted to."

"What do they look like?"

Isabelle put her hand over her heart. "They look like rag mops with eyes, except that you can barely tell they have eyes because of their fur. They're crazy looking. I am in love with each one of them. You have to come with me to pick one out."

"Sure. I'll come." Suddenly she saw Isabelle's life as uncomplicated. Isabelle didn't have to worry about a phone call from someone that Grace wanted to get a call from. All of Isabelle's energy was focused on a little pile of mop that would be her shadow. Then Margaret felt guilty for thinking of Isabelle's life as uncomplicated, because Isabelle's father was dead, and a puppy wouldn't make up for all that Isabelle had been through and still carried. But a puppy would be sweet. Why didn't her own mother ever offer her a puppy?

"Does Grace know?"

"No, but I'll tell her after school."

"Did you know that Grace had a dog named Crackers when she was little?"

"No."

"Grace's brother Chuck was little, too, and Crackers bit Chuck when Chuck was eating Crackers's supper. That was the end of Crackers."

"Where did he go?"

"Somebody's grandparents."

"You won't eat my puppy's food, will you, Margaret?"

"I can't promise."

"It's funny, isn't it?" said Isabelle. "My dog isn't a job or a boyfriend or a car, but I'm so happy about him or her. I feel fluttery in my stomach just thinking about it."

Margaret felt fluttery in her chest when she thought about Teddy, but the idea of talking to or seeing him put her stomach in the mind of diarrhea.

They walked for another half block before Francine—a friendly junior—emerged from the alley between Pleasant and Pillsbury Avenues. Relief swept over Margaret. It would be harder to worry about Teddy issues with someone besides Isabelle present. Francine fell in step with Margaret and Isabelle.

"Isabelle is getting a puppy," said Margaret. "A young mop."

"You're lucky," said Francine. "My parents won't consider it. When do you get yours?"

"As soon as it doesn't need a mom," Isabelle said.

"You'll be the mom," said Francine. "But who's going to let it out and stuff when you're gone? I know your mother teaches."

Isabelle had arrived in Minneapolis years earlier without a father or siblings—almost unheard of at a Catholic school.

"Our landlady," she said. "She lives downstairs, so that's where the puppy will be on school days. And the backyard is fenced."

"She must be a really nice landlady."

"She misses her sister—her sister died—so the puppy will be company for Miss Flora. Except on Saturday and Sunday. And summer vacation."

"How will the puppy know it's your dog and not the landlady's?" Francine asked.

"She'll just know. She'll sleep upstairs in my room."

"Isabelle, you said 'she,'" said Margaret. "So it's a girl?"

"I don't know why I said that. It doesn't matter one bit."

A puppy that would sleep in your room—Isabelle didn't know how lucky she was, Margaret thought. It was uncomplicated. Of course, potty training could be intense, she knew. Even with that, a puppy that peed on the floor occasionally was a piece of cake compared to the Teddy problem. But *if* Teddy called, *if* he asked her out, she would never, never go, and the reason was one word: Grace. Solved. How had that happened in one second, feeling certain and free? And why was she thinking about this when Francine was talking?

"It will be so much fun to name the puppy," Francine said. "Hamlet. Ophelia. Old Yeller."

"Sherman? Bongo? Princess Margaret?" said Margaret. "This could take a lifetime."

How fun would it be to have a little puppy across the street—pure joy rather than the burden of carrying Teddy around like a headache. Teddy, out of sight, out of mind, she pledged to herself. Focus on the puppy.

6

"The phone's for you," Mark yelled on Saturday morning, pounding on the first-floor door to the upstairs with the two rooms and sloped ceiling. Margaret's brother dreaded going up there since the time Margaret had chased him back down when he showed up uninvited. Margaret had been combing her hair and, while chasing Mark, tripped on the stairs and jammed the comb's pointy handle into the roof of her mouth. After she recovered from the pain, she tried to stab Mark with the handle while he tried to find safety behind their mother.

Margaret squinted at the alarm clock, which told her that it was ten forty.

"Say that I'll call back." She pulled the covers over her head.

"I don't know who it is."

"Ask." What was worse, having Mark for a meddlesome brother or sharing the upstairs with twins whose favorite activity was pawing through her jewelry box when she wasn't home?

"It's a man."

A man. She didn't know any men. If it were a baby-sitting request, either Mrs. O'Connor or Mrs. Solforth would call, not a husband. Margaret squeezed her eyes to keep the sun out.

"I am not here. I don't know a man."

Her eyes flashed open. Was Teddy a man?

The floor was cold. Where were her slippers? Forget it. She ran—her only thought was to reach the phone and make the man go away.

Mark followed her into the dining room. Margaret gave him her most soul-shattering glare as she picked up the receiver, covering the mouthpiece with her hand.

"Okay, okay," he said. "It's not like I'm interested in your life."

Mercifully, her mother was in the basement, consorting with the laundry, and her father was waxing the car; Margaret could see him through the dining room windows.

The telephone had never felt so ominous.

"Hello?"

"Hey, Margaret, it's Teddy from the Emerald. Grace's friend. How's it going?"

Going? Not well.

"It's going." She wished that she had hung up before speaking.

Teddy laughed as if she had said something clever. "Hey, do you want to do something tonight?"

One of the twins turned up the volume on the television in the living room. Cartoons, the lifeblood of her sisters.

Do something? No, she didn't want to do something. "I can't," she heard herself say.

"Hey, why not?"

"I'm babysitting." She wasn't.

"Could I drop by?"

Was he kidding? Drop over when she was babysitting? She could lose her job, couldn't she? Then she remembered that she wasn't babysitting.

"I can't have friends over," she said.

"Well, at least you consider me a friend. Or a friend's friend? That counts. So what have you been up to?"

"Nothing."

"I doubt that. Let's go out next weekend. Don't take any babysitting gigs for Saturday."

"I'll have to look at my calendar." She didn't have a calendar. "My mom is calling. I have to go."

"I'll call back. Soon. Don't put too many babies on that calendar. See you."

She hung up and stared at the phone. Five minutes ago it had been a cherished conduit to everyone she loved most—Grace, Isabelle, Grandma, librarians who took renewals over the phone. Now Teddy's deep and hearty voice resonated. She needed to talk to Grace. But Grace was the last person in the world she could talk to about Teddy's call. She could call Isabelle, but that would be going behind Grace's back.

She heard a moan. It was hers. She wanted a puppy—like the one Isabelle would soon have—to bury her face in because her own hands weren't comforting like puppy fur.

Because she didn't know what to do about Teddy, she went upstairs and dressed. Downstairs, the phone rang. Please, God, don't let it be Teddy. She ran back down so that she would beat Mark to it, or her mother, who would run up from the basement if no one else answered. The twins wouldn't care if it rang all day.

She looked outside. Spring was lagging behind, the ground still covered with a few shaded patches of gray snow drizzled with yellow urine, courtesy of neighborhood dogs. Margaret put her hand on the phone but did not pick it up. Would she run away if it were warmer? Would it be worth dropping out of high school before she completed her third year? She pictured Teddy but wished that she could remove the white butcher's cap from his head to see if he was hiding anything, like a crew cut or devil horns. Maybe, just maybe, it would be a little bit fun to go out with him. Why was she afraid? Would Grace really be hurt?

The phone rang.

She heard her mother open the door at the top of the basement stairs.

"I'm getting it, I'm getting it," Margaret yelled.

Before she had uttered the second syllable of "hello," she heard Grace say, "You'll never guess what happened to me."

"What?" Maybe Teddy had realized that he had made a mistake. Maybe he had called Grace and asked her out because she was funny and could talk to anyone, and because she really, really liked him, and because, in a certain light, her hair was like pale oranges and strawberries streaked together.

"My mom said I could take driver's ed if I pay for it. My dad works too much overtime to teach me."

"Why can't your mom teach you?"

"From the couch? Besides, who wants to learn to drive like my mom?"

"How will you pay?"

"Excuse me. I work for a living. I'll just have to cut back on the Screaming Yellow Zonkers I put in my lunch."

"Grace, your mother will let you take the car after you get your license?"

"That was her brother's old car. She borrowed it for a long time. Seven years? His insurance was high because of accidents. He took a break."

"So what will you drive?"

"Maybe my dad's when he doesn't need it. I should go study the little book for my learner's permit. My dad brought one home."

"You know all the rules. I heard you tell your mother what the speed limit is in the alley."

"I just like to say it: learner's permit. What are you doing tonight?"

"Babysitting. I mean, I'm not babysitting. Let's go to Isabelle's. I think her mom is going out with that park police guy."

"Still going out with him? How can she go out with someone so old?"

"Grace, he's younger than she is."

"What I mean is, why would old people date?"

"I don't know, but Isabelle likes it because her mom likes it."

"Anyway, I wish that she had her puppy," Grace said. "We could teach it tricks. Dancing on its hind legs. Barking twice for yes, one for no."

"Have you ever done that?"

"No, but I could."

She probably could, Margaret thought. "Okay, I'll tell Isabelle that we'll be there around seven o'clock."

"Tell her that I'm going to name the puppy."

"I'll tell her to hide the puppy so that you don't steal it."

Margaret hung up. What a terrible beginning

to the day—and what a relief it was to hear Grace's voice. Grace anchored things even though she wasn't always anchored. She would tell Grace about Teddy's call. Of course she would. She wasn't going out with him. Ever.

7

Isabelle's mother had left before Margaret and Grace arrived on Saturday evening.

"Look at what Miss Flora brought for us," said Isabelle, as Margaret and Grace followed her to the kitchen.

"She should open a bakery," Grace said. "She seems to have time on her hands."

"It's so tall," Margaret said. "Four layers?" The creamy frosting with little swirls put Margaret in the mind of pin curls, swirls of hair anchored to the head with bobby pins. Her mother used to set her hair—and Margaret's—on Saturday evenings.

"What should we do before *Gunsmoke* comes on?" Grace asked, her finger circling the bottom of the cake plate.

"Do you still watch it every week when you're not with us?" Isabelle asked.

"You would, too, if it was one of the few times during the week that peace reigned in your house."

Sometimes Margaret worried a little about Isabelle. Did too much peace reign in her house? A puppy couldn't replace her father, but maybe it could liven things up.

"We could talk about my job," said Grace, as she lowered herself to the carpet and stretched out on her side, her hand holding up her head.

"We already know about your job," said Margaret. "So what's new about it?"

"Teddy."

The air supply to Margaret's brain ceased. The gray matter did not register thought.

"Teddy?" Isabelle asked. "Are you going out with him?"

"Nice try. He's going out with someone else."

"Why would he tell you?" Isabelle said.

"Because he's a jerk?"

"Is it someone at work?"

"Okay. I exaggerated. He told me that he's trying to get someone to go out with him. She's playing hard to get, he said."

"Why would he tell you?"

"He probably pulls legs off frogs. I don't know and I wish he'd go away."

Margaret knew that she was still alive because she had a thought that had been taking up space in her head since Teddy had called. Secrets burn a hole in your heart, she had read somewhere.

It would not be so complicated if Teddy hadn't sounded so confident, if Grace wasn't involved, if

Mark never hovered, if she didn't want her mother to know anything.

This was the moment to tell Grace. Then the hole forming in her heart would heal.

An image of Teddy interrupted the thought of her heart healing. He was so cute and handsome at the same time. He appeared self-confident. He was full of bluster, unlike anyone she knew except Grace. What could he see in her, Margaret, that she didn't see? A girl who would understand him better than anyone because she didn't talk about herself continuously? He had never talked to her before today. A nice enough–looking girl after she ironed her hair and used blusher and mascara? But she hadn't been wearing any makeup when he saw her. A possible girlfriend? He knew nothing about her.

Isabelle straightened her spine. "I know," she said. "Let's go to Harley's house and see the puppies."

"What about the cake?" asked Grace.

"Nobody's going to eat it while we're gone."

"Can we go over there and demand to see them?" Margaret asked. "Can we just barge in on a Saturday night?"

"Why not?" Isabelle said, sounding Grace-like. "One of those puppies is mine."

"Harley?" Isabelle said after dialing. "This is Isabelle, Mrs. Day's daughter. Would your parents mind if I brought my friends over to see the puppies for a minute?" Isabelle smiled at Margaret and Grace as she listened to Harley.

"Great!" she said into the receiver. "We won't stay long."

She hung up the phone. "There's a babysitter over there," Isabelle said. "Harley said she doesn't care. Here we go."

8

Twilight bathed them on the walk to Harley's, and the air was damp with spring.

Harley opened the front door of his house on Garfield Avenue. The babysitter was parked on the carpet in front of *Get Smart*. Four children younger than Harley sprawled on the living room floor in different stages of consciousness. A diapered baby lay on its back, frustrated that its mouth couldn't quite catch its toes. A toddler slumped, her head drooping almost into her lap. The other two were squishing Play-Doh into the carpet. The babysitter glanced at Grace, Isabelle, and Margaret.

"Hey, Grace," she said. "Looks like you're having about as much fun as I am tonight."

"More, Janet," Grace said. "It's my night off."

"The puppies are in the kitchen," said Harley.

"Who's the babysitter?" Isabelle asked Grace as they walked down a hall.

"She's a senior at Central. A cheerleader. I thought she was out every night of the week with her boyfriend. Who knew?"

"Janet made dinner," Harley said. "She's supposed to clean up." Dirty plates rested haphazardly on the counter; hot dogs floated in a pan on the stove.

"Why don't you clean up?" Grace said. "You look old enough."

"I'm nine," said Harley. "It's not my job."

"When I was your age, I had a baby on each hip while I was ironing clothes in the bathroom so I could keep an eye on the toddlers in the tub."

"Is that a bit of an exaggeration, Grace?" Isabelle said.

"No, it's an understatement. I was peeling potatoes with my third hand."

Harley frowned at Grace.

"She's always like this," Isabelle said.

"I like your mom," Harley said to Isabelle. "She's my favorite teacher."

"I'll tell her. It will make her happy."

Harley looked pleased with himself. "Do you want to hold the puppies?"

Grace was already inspecting them as they attempted to climb out of their ramshackle pen made of wooden fruit cartons.

"Why can't we take one now?" Grace asked.

Harley plucked a puppy, whose legs scrambled to find traction in the air. "They still need their mom. This one is mine." He positioned the puppy so that its paws were on his chest. The puppy jerked its head back and stared at Harley as if it had never noticed that Harley had a face. Then it lunged at Harley's cheek, apparently with intent to lap it up.

"I named him Licorice because he loves to lick my face," said Harley. "His short name is Lik."

Grace reached down for a puppy, which danced in the air as it was pulled upward. "This one is all personality, like me."

"They look like cocker spaniels and labs and terriers or something, all mixed up," Isabelle said. "How can you choose just one? Impossible."

"They're mutts," said Harley. "Like their mom."

Isabelle pointed to the smallest one, whose sisters and brothers used his head as a walkway.

"Why, Isabelle?" asked Margaret.

"He bounces back."

"From being pummeled?" Grace asked.

"He's not upset," Isabelle said. "He's not in a hurry to go somewhere for the sake of going there." She moved the crates enough to put one leg in the makeshift pen and reach to the back.

"Is it a boy or girl?" Grace asked. "Boys are trouble."

"I'm not trouble," Harley said.

"In five years I'm going to ask your parents where you are, and they'll say, 'Oh, Harley? He's in trouble.'"

Harley snorted.

"Snorting at adults is a sure sign that you're headed for trouble," said Grace.

"You're not an adult." Harley began to walk out of the kitchen. "And that puppy's a boy."

"I really don't care," said Isabelle, as the puppy stared at her.

"What's its name?" Grace asked.

"I'm not sure." The puppy licked Isabelle's chin.

"Call him Teddy," said Grace.

"You don't want to name him Teddy," Margaret said.

"It's a sweet name, Margaret," said Isabelle. "Teddy Bear."

"Theodore," said Grace. "Theodore Roosevelt, president of our country in olden times. Theodor Geisel, also known as Dr. Seuss. Don't forget the Chipmunks—Alvin, Simon, and Theodore."

"But why would you want such a sappy name for such a darling puppy?" Margaret needed to convince Isabelle. "It's a stupid name."

"It's funny," Grace said. "It's a great name for a dog."

"I love it," said Isabelle. "My own Teddy Bear."

"There's something weird about it," Margaret said. "You can do better."

"If Grace doesn't mind being reminded of that rat Teddy, I don't mind," Isabelle said.

How could this be happening? For the rest of her life—or Teddy the puppy's life—she, Margaret, would be reminded of the "man" on the phone and her mistake in not telling Grace immediately.

"Teddy, Teddy, Teddy, you'll soon be ours," Grace crooned.

"It's a stupid name," Margaret said.

Harley returned to the kitchen for a banana Popsicle.

"Hey, Trouble, when can we take our puppy home?" Grace asked.

"I told you. They still need their mom. Maybe a week? We get to keep one of them, and the mom, Tipsy. But I decided to change Lik's name."

"To what?"

Harley screwed up his face at Grace. "Chuckle-head."

"Why Chucklehead?"

"After you."

Grace lowered her face to Harley's level. "Let's trade names," she said. "I'm more about trouble and you're the Chucklehead."

"Time to go," said Margaret.

Harley looked at Isabelle. "Tell your mom that your friend is a nutcase."

"As soon as I get home. Thanks for letting us come over and see Teddy."

"At least you're the owner," Harley said, pointing at Grace. "That girl is crazy."

"Believe it," Grace said, as she walked to the front door, Margaret and Isabelle behind her. The curved slice of moon shone brightly.

"This night is perfect," said Isabelle. "Little Teddy, spring, us. Perfect."

"My only concern is Teddy's welfare," said Grace. "I can't have my own Teddy—the puppy, I mean— because Bernadette wouldn't care for him while I'm at school or work. But I might find a high school that allows dogs. I can hear the principal, 'Teddy, you and Grace came in first in the talent show.' What a team. Teddy will lick my face, confirming that I am more than a lovely parent, I'm a patient and accomplished trainer. The next . . ."

"Prattle," Margaret said, turning to look at Grace. "That's what you do. Prattle, prattle, prattle." She pulled ahead on the sidewalk.

"That's what we do," said Grace in a very loud voice. "What do you want to talk about? World peace?"

Irritation flooded Margaret as she picked up her pace. She didn't care if she ever saw Grace again. At least not for a day or two.

9

Margaret pushed the bathroom door open between second and third periods. Where did the custodians and the seminarians that sometimes taught religion class go to the bathroom? Third year of high school and she had never seen a door marked "Men."

Daisy Winter, a junior, pouted in front of a mirror as she brushed her honey-blond tresses, so heavy that her hair looked like an entity rather than individual strands. "I *hate* my hair," she said as she brushed, her eyes caressing her reflection. "I *hate* it."

Margaret pushed a stall door open, wondering if Daisy talked to her hair frequently or only when an audience was present. When she looked at Daisy, she saw hair. What did people see when they saw her?

She bent her head and used the metal sanitary napkin disposal as a cloudy mirror. Nothing was wrong with her: round eyes, a few freckles, no zits. Would she want Daisy Winter's hair, all of it? No. How could it come without an attitude?

She waited until she heard Daisy leave, then proceeded to the sink. Next class, English. Yesterday

Sister Cleopha had talked about the author Thomas Hardy with intimacy in her voice. His poetry should have been as highly acclaimed as his prose, she said. After all, he considered himself a poet first, then a novelist. Either way his name had been plastered on required reading throughout eternity, Margaret thought. A lot of the girls complained bitterly about *The Mayor of Casterbridge,* but Margaret reveled in the gloom.

Not only was English the best class, but it was the only class she shared with Isabelle. And Sister Cleopha, like Señorita Waters, was one of the very kind teachers. Unlike Sister Ursuline, the other English teacher, she didn't try to scare her homeroom students by warning them about the dangers of intimacy with a boyfriend. Francine told Margaret and Isabelle that Sister Ursuline had said, "Imagine putting something the circumference of a silver dollar in your canal, your private area. Well, the male part is much too large for that. Dwell on it." Francine wasn't the only one who wondered how Sister had acquired this information.

When the girls walked home after school, there was one topic.

"Do you think you might get the puppy this weekend?" Francine asked Isabelle.

"We hope so."

"We think of it as our dog," Margaret said. "I'm so close that I almost live in the same house."

"Just think how much fun it would be if you could have one of the puppies, too," Isabelle said.

"You know, my mom."

"What about your mom?" Francine said.

"My mom would never let me have a puppy or any pet. She spends most of her time trying to make the house look like no one lives in it."

"A lot of housewives do that," said Francine. "We have a dish of hard candy on the coffee table, but we're not allowed to eat it."

"You have Fred, don't you?" Isabelle said. "He must have been a puppy."

"I was an only child for a while, and my mom thought that having a dog would make me more normal. In dog years, he was grown up, so he didn't eat shoes and books or anything."

"Your mom sounds nice," said Margaret.

"Your mom is, too," said Francine. "When we were in grade school, she always made cookies for you to pass out on your birthday."

"Most of them—the moms—try, I guess," said Margaret. "Isabelle's mom is *so* nice." She paused. "Grace's mom is something else."

As soon as she said it, she wished that she hadn't. She was trying not to think about Grace. They hadn't talked since Saturday night at Harley's.

10

Monday night was a good night. Teddy didn't call. He didn't call on Tuesday either, or Wednesday or Thursday. Every day Margaret felt lighter. But like a burr in her shoe, the idea that he might expect to see her on Saturday was hard to ignore.

While they waited on the corner for Francine after school on Friday, Isabelle said, "Grace wants to stay overnight on Saturday if we bring the puppy home."

Have I ever gone six days without talking to Grace? Margaret wondered. Even when she was on vacation—sleeping in campgrounds that didn't have indoor plumbing so that everyone in the family could eventually peer into the Grand Canyon or some other place that didn't have indoor plumbing—she sent postcards to Grace, postcards on which her writing was so small that it looked like mites on paper. That had to serve as communication until she got home and they would talk over everything that had transpired during their two weeks apart.

"I know I can," said Margaret.

"My mom likes it when my friends come over."

The girls walked past the drive-in. The sun was out, and so was everyone who had driven there, leaning on their cars and anyone else's.

"It must be seventy degrees," said Isabelle. "When it's seventy, I can't feel the air touch my skin because my skin and the air are one entity."

"Isabelle, you are poetic," Francine said.

It was true, Margaret thought. Isabelle was showing signs of what she, Margaret, now wanted to be. Was that okay? There was probably room for two more poets in the world. When Sister Cleopha had talked about Emily Dickinson, she said that Isabelle's writing showed the sensitivity of a poet. Suzanne Uphill's hair, Sister said, was in the style of Emily Dickinson's, and Margaret's hair was the same color as the poet's, as if Sister had a lock of Emily's hair in a box in a bureau in her nun's cell. Margaret felt a little cheated because she harbored a passion to be a poet rather than someone with the same color hair as a poet, although not in the same style.

"Have you noticed that car that's driving very slowly across the street from us?" Francine asked.

"It's probably somebody who's taking driver's ed," said Margaret. A state testing center sat across from the school on the east side of Fourth Avenue. "I cannot wait to see the puppy, Isabelle." She didn't bother to look at the car.

The car's driver made a U-turn in the street.

"Are you still going to name him Teddy?" asked Francine. No one bothered with the car that was traveling at about three miles per hour next to them.

"That is *so* cute. I can't stand how cute that name is for that puppy."

Margaret glanced at the car. Someone was leaning toward the passenger door, one hand remaining on the steering wheel. It looked like Teddy, the one who was not a puppy. The car crept along, continuing at a speed that she could outwalk. Margaret walked faster.

"Hey, girls, want a ride home?"

Margaret looked over her shoulder at Teddy, who had stopped the car and emerged from it. "No," she said.

"Where did that cute guy come from?" asked Francine.

"He works at the Emerald with Grace." In an uncharacteristically loud voice, Isabelle called to Teddy. "Grace doesn't go to school with us. She's at Central."

"I know. I was just on my way to the drive-in and saw you walking."

"Why not take a ride?" Francine asked. "He must be okay if he knows Grace."

"I like to walk." Margaret sped up her pace. "And you live only two blocks from here."

"We never get a ride, Margaret," Isabelle said, as she tried to catch up with her.

Margaret wanted to scream at her. The scream would mean: Do you know what he did behind Grace's back? He is slime, exceptionally slimy slime. Grace likes him, and he must know that.

Instead, she said, "It's kind of weird that he's hanging around a high school. He looks old."

"He's adorable," Francine said.

"Just keep walking," said Margaret. "Don't look back."

"Okay," Teddy called. "Just thought you girls might like a ride home."

He waved as he drove past them. Francine was the only one who waved back.

After Francine turned left at her corner, Isabelle said to Margaret, "I wonder why he's hanging around school."

"Got me."

As usual, the twins were home before Margaret. Their school—formerly Margaret's—was half the distance of the high school.

"Will you play Monopoly with us?" Kathleen asked.

Margaret felt a sudden mist in her eyes. The twins were so innocent. What was the most challenging situation they faced? Who got to lick the beater with the most batter on it when Mom made a cake?

"I'm going to sleep over at Isabelle's tonight, but we can start a game before supper and finish it tomorrow."

Kathleen, whose expectations were usually low, stared as if she couldn't process Margaret's words. Karen walked into the dining room. "Margaret is going to play Monopoly with us," Kathleen said.

Karen looked hard at Kathleen, then Margaret. "Why?"

"Because our sister asked me," she said. All these years of living with the twins, and I know how to stop them in their tracks: agree to something.

"Stay here," said Kathleen. "Both of you." She ran to get Monopoly from the games cupboard upstairs and ran back. "Let's set it up in the living room."

Margaret moved slowly. The sight of Teddy had drained her. He had come too close.

"Remember, I have to leave right after supper," Margaret said as she counted out the Monopoly money and distributed it.

"We won't play until you get back," Kathleen said. "We'll keep playing tomorrow." She chose the Scottie dog as her piece.

"I want the little iron," said Karen.

I want to be a little girl again, Margaret said to herself.

The phone rang. It did not sound like a call Margaret wanted, although it was no different from any other ring. Mark ran from the kitchen and plucked it out of its cradle. "She's here," he said. "She's always here."

Margaret moved to grab the phone that Mark held in the air, and they each pulled on one end of it. For just a flash, whoever was on the line was irrelevant. Margaret fought for the phone so that she could pound Mark on the head with it.

"Maybe I'm waiting for a call," Mark screamed as he struggled.

"Stop fighting over me," said the voice on the phone said. "I don't want anyone to bleed on my account."

Mark glared at Margaret as he shoved the phone into her stomach. Margaret tried to wither him with a hateful stare.

"Grace," she said into the phone.

"Just confirming that I'll be at Isabelle's as soon as I finish the dishes."

"I'm almost done playing Monopoly with the twins."

"*Twilight Zone.* Bring your pillow."

"Sure."

"One of Isabelle's outstanding qualities is that there aren't any little kids at her house."

"Grace, do you ever wish you were little again?"

"No. Remember, after I was born my mom kept

having babies so that I'd have something to do. I was never little."

"See you soon." Margaret hung up the phone. She wanted to be with Grace, Grace who had an answer for everything. Then again, she wanted to avoid her. It was a first.

11

"No *Twilight Zone* tonight," Isabelle said to Margaret at the door.

"Why are you grinning like an idiot, and why can't we watch *Twilight Zone*?"

"Come and see."

The entrance to the kitchen was blocked by what looked like the top of an old desk. Isabelle's mom and Miss Flora McCarthy sat in the kitchen, coffee cups on the table.

Little Teddy was attempting to climb the barricade. He jumped high enough so that his face appeared momentarily before he fell backward, repeatedly.

"Oh, Isabelle," was all that Margaret could say. How had she ever lived without encountering anything this perfect? He had been perfect one week ago, but seeing him in Isabelle's kitchen, attempting to levitate on a linoleum floor marked by puppy urine, Margaret was besotted once again.

"My mom picked him up right after her school got out," Isabelle said. "She and her friend Teresa brought him home before I got here. Pick him up, Margaret."

Margaret leaned over and lifted Teddy. His bottom sank into her arms as he quivered and frantically sniffed her face.

"Mine," said Margaret. "He's mine."

"Oh, my dear," said Miss Flora. "I'm sure that you will have your own Teddy in time."

Was Miss Flora a psychic? Why did she have to be reminded of the lesser Teddy during this moment of pure, uncompromised joy?

"Let's bring him into the living room," Isabelle said.

"I miss him already," said Miss Flora, as she snuggled her hands into the sleeves of her cardigan sweater.

"You'll have him every school day of the year," Isabelle said. "You'll have all those days to spoil him with brownies and other treats poisonous to puppies."

"Everyone needs to be spoiled sometimes. Do you girls want some blueberry pie?" She nodded to the pie in front of her on the table. "There's another one in my kitchen if there isn't enough."

"We'll have some later," said Isabelle. "After Margaret and Grace have some time with Teddy."

In the morning, Margaret woke up on Isabelle's bedroom floor with something moist—like a damp pencil eraser—inspecting her face. It seemed to be trembling. She opened her eyes to see two small dark ones staring back.

"Oh, Teddy," she said to the puppy, who commenced licking her face.

"It's almost noon," Isabelle said. "We didn't think you'd mind being woken up. My mom kept Teddy in the kitchen last night in his little dog bed. With a blanket."

Little Teddy cocked his head when Isabelle spoke.

"Why does your bed look as if you didn't sleep in it?" said Margaret.

"She spent the night with Teddy," Grace said.

Teddy stared at Grace as a stream of urine pooled beneath him.

"We have to house-train the little guy," said Isabelle.

"Obviously." Grace sat on the floor, fully dressed. "I have to show up for work today, so I can't stay and help you."

"How's that Teddy at work?" Isabelle asked.

"Alive. He has no interest in me whatsoever. That's so weird that he wanted to give you guys a ride home. He doesn't even live around here."

Isabelle must have told Grace about the offer.

Margaret's stomach signaled that it wanted to be alone, where breakfast could roil around in it privately.

Little Teddy stood still as one ear twitched, then tore out of the room as if being called by someone no one else could hear.

"I guess potty training will be intense," said Margaret. "But I have to go home and vacuum up invisible stuff now."

"You can't eat breakfast?"

"Okay, but I have to hustle."

"Me, too," said Grace. "I can't believe that Bernadette hasn't sent out a posse to collect me."

Margaret left first. How old do you have to be to get an apartment? she wondered as she crossed the street. And a phone with an unlisted number? And why do I worry about things that haven't happened? Teddy has not called back.

12

Vacuuming in the dining room when the phone rang, Margaret answered before she recognized what she had done.

"Hey, Margaret," said Teddy. "I'm at my cousin's house. You know him, Marty Hennings."

She had graduated from eighth grade with Marty Hennings. He was related to Teddy?

"He's my little cousin. Big cousin's here, too, but I found out that Marty knows you."

Margaret didn't remember Martin fondly. What was she supposed to say? Does Martin know about deodorant yet?

"We're coming over to pick you up for lunch."

Clutching the vacuum, Margaret inadvertently switched it on. Jolted, she fumbled to turn it off. But Teddy had hung up before she had time to say no. How could she tell him that she wanted nothing to do with him? She would be forced to tell him in person, if he really came over. She pictured him without intending to: a swaggering, self-assured blowhard in a butcher's cap. Phlegm blossomed in her throat as she pictured his mouth, smiling a little too eagerly.

She didn't comb her hair or change into a clean T-shirt or put her shoes on. Running to the front door, she yelled, "Going to Isabelle's." The twin faces, glued to cartoons, didn't move. She charged out the front door, and the cool air bit her. Within minutes, Teddy's car turned the corner and traveled from Thirty-Eighth Street to her. It stopped, engine running. Teddy's arm reached for the passenger door and opened it. Rather than stand outside and appear conspicuous, Margaret entered, one knee at time, so that she knelt on the passenger seat and looked slightly down on Teddy.

"Do not ever call me again," she said. "I do not like you. Goodbye." She scanned the back seat. "Where's Martin?"

"He couldn't come."

"Is he really your cousin?"

"Of course. Sheldon and Dolores are my uncle and aunt. Check it out."

Through the window on the driver's side, Margaret saw Isabelle across the street, holding Little Teddy on a leash, staring. Each of Little Teddy's feet was scrambling without making any progress. Margaret stared back. Could Isabelle see that she, Margaret—innocent and kneeling—was silently begging for help?

"We have to talk," Teddy said. "Just a few minutes, by the lake." He peeled away from the curb. "Close your door, please."

"You're kidnapping me," Margaret said, as she tugged the door handle. "I don't know you, so you're a kidnapper."

"Margaret, I am Teddy. I am not kidnapping you. Do you want to get out here?" He pulled over to the curb on Dupont, next to the cemetery.

She opened the door and got out, but to her horror, Teddy got out as well. He walked around the back of the car and stood next to her.

"I don't know you very well, at all," he said. "But I keep thinking about you. You're so nice. I mean, you seem like a very nice person. Some other people are nice, I'm sure, but I noticed you. I think you're different, in a good way."

"Oh," said Margaret.

"Now, if you want to kneel in my car again, I'll take you home. But I want you to think about going out with me."

"I'll walk home. I'm almost home already."

Teddy put his hand on her shoulder, and Margaret remembered the shock she had felt when she put a butter knife in a socket at age three.

"Will you think about what I said?"

"I can't go out with you." Teddy's hand was still electrocuting her so that it was difficult to talk. "I can't go out with you because of Grace." Teddy's face looked smooth. There wasn't any gross stubble on it.

"I never went out with Grace. So why does it matter?" he asked.

"She likes you."

"My mom likes me, too, but she doesn't care if I go out with you." Teddy looked concerned.

"Grace is my best friend, the friend I've had for the longest time in my life. But Isabelle is my best friend, too. I knew Grace before I knew Isabelle because I met Grace in first grade, and Isabelle moved here when I was in eighth grade, and now she lives right across the street—kitty-corner, actually."

Teddy was staring at her, listening. Did he understand?

"So I don't want to hurt Grace's feelings, because she likes you," Margaret continued.

"Do you want me to talk to her?" Teddy asked.

Was he crazy? What could he say to Grace? "I have two choices and you're the loser?"

"No."

"Do you want me to meet your parents as long as we're a block from your house?"

"No." She watched a car approaching from the south on Dupont Avenue. A hand waved from the passenger side as the car turned the corner: Miss Flora, returning from her weekly trip to Foodtown and a drive around Lake Harriet with her daughter.

Margaret lifted her hand in response, wishing that Miss Flora would tell her daughter to stop and rescue her younger neighbor.

"Okay," Teddy said. "But could we go out sometime?"

"You're too old. My parents wouldn't like that." If they met him, they would see that Teddy was possibly an adult.

"I thought that Grace was the obstacle."

Why didn't he drive back to wherever he came from?

"Okay, okay," she said. If she told him that she would meet him, he'd go away. He could wait forever, and she would never show up. That would stop him from bothering her.

"I'll meet you at the park at six thirty."

Margaret felt emboldened by her plan. She might as well know how old he was, so she asked.

"Twenty," he said. "How old are you?"

"Seventeen," she said. There was no half yet.

"I don't want to make this hard for you," Teddy said. "I think I should meet your parents."

"No, that won't be necessary." Margaret said as she turned her back on him and walked away. Her relief at having a plan—or a non-plan—made her so giddy that she turned and smiled at Teddy.

"See you at six thirty," he called to her back.

Isabelle was sitting on her front steps with Little Teddy as Margaret crossed the street.

"I know that was Teddy," said Isabelle. "At first I couldn't believe it, but then I saw those dice hanging from his rearview mirror. I noticed them when he tried to give us a ride home from school."

Margaret felt a flicker of resentment as she looked at Isabelle. Isabelle's only problem was how to train Little Teddy so that he wouldn't ruin all the floors in the duplex and make it smell like an outhouse.

They sat and watched Little Teddy, whose excitement over a patch of dead leaves had no limits.

"There must be dinosaur bones under there," Margaret said.

"Or a roast beef."

The girls continued to watch Little Teddy dig frantically.

"You're wondering why I got in the car," said Margaret.

"I'm wondering how he knows where you live."

"Somehow Teddy found out that his cousin and I were in grade school together, you know, Martin Hennings. So Teddy must have looked up my address and number in the phone book."

"That's weird."

"Anyway, he called and said that he was coming

over, so I ran out to tell him to leave. But somehow, I was in the car and he was driving it."

"Then what?"

"He tried to take me to the lake, but I made him stop on Dupont, and he said I was nice and he wants to go out with me. Then Miss Flora's daughter drove by with Miss Flora. The end."

Isabelle stared at Margaret and, enunciating her words with deliberation, said, "Tell Grace."

"Tell Grace what?"

"Tell her what happened. Just like you always tell her everything that happens."

"She'll be upset. She likes him."

"Maybe she'll be upset or maybe she won't. You can't do anything about that."

Margaret looked at Isabelle's shoes. They were her mother's loafers, not hers. She knew Grace's shoes, too, but she didn't know what she needed to know about her now. It was impossible to guess Grace's reaction.

"What if she's really, really angry?" Margaret asked.

"It's better than not telling her."

"But they've never gone out."

"Doesn't matter," Isabelle said. "It's killing you."

"You're wearing your mom's shoes. Is that why you sound like a mom?"

"I'm just saying out loud what you know, Margaret. Now dial."

Grace answered her phone. As usual, there was a din in the background—her brothers and sisters always filling the space with noise in the absence of a mother who would direct them to do something more positive than bicker over who had eaten the last packets of Kool-Aid.

Isabelle watched Margaret as if Margaret might make a break for the door.

"Grace, I have something to tell you," Margaret said. She looked at Isabelle as if Isabelle might release her from this trial.

"So, tell me."

With her eyes, Margaret pleaded with Isabelle for help.

"I'm with Isabelle, at her house."

"Is that going to be on the news tonight?"

"Be serious, Grace. I'm trying to tell you something. That Teddy person asked me out."

Silence.

"I said no."

Silence.

"He came over in his car today, and I didn't want him here."

Margaret listened to Grace exhale loudly. "I don't

care if you go out with that creep or anyone else," Grace said, her voice tight and pitched a little higher than usual.

This is like going to confession, Margaret thought. She was asking forgiveness for something that she was beginning to think she wanted to do.

"Really, Grace? You wouldn't have cared?" She was begging for absolution. "Anyway, I told him no."

"You already said that. But why would I care?" asked Grace, her voice rising. "The more I see him, the more I know I'd never go out with him. He is definitely not my type."

Margaret didn't want to spoil the moment by asking Grace what her type was.

"Grace, I don't want anything to mess us up, I mean, come between us. Ever."

"This will not. Anyway, you basically kicked him in the teeth, right?"

"Right." Not really.

"This doesn't change anything between us."

"Right." How could she lie so blatantly? The more that Grace used a steely tone, the more Margaret wondered why she was telling her that she didn't want to go out with Teddy. She just didn't want Grace to be mad at her.

"Okay, then. Nothing happened."

"Nothing happened."

When Margaret hung up the phone, she didn't

feel any better. Something beneath Grace's denial lingered.

She and Isabelle climbed through Isabelle's bedroom window onto the flat roof. The birch tree branches swayed a little, gently slapping the roof's edge.

"Did you ever think of jumping to that tree's trunk and climbing down?" Margaret asked. "Running away?"

"When I thought of escaping—you know, going back to my other life that was already over in Milwaukee—I thought of using the front door. If I had been younger, maybe I would have thought of something dramatic. But that trunk doesn't look too sturdy." She paused. "You know, we could sleep out here tonight if you want to."

"That would be fun except that I'd be afraid that I'd roll off in my sleep."

"It's possible."

"I could still stay over," Margaret said. But the comfort of being with Isabelle dissolved as she continued. "I told Teddy that I'd meet him at the park. I have to figure out how to do that. So I'll tell my mom that I'm staying over here, okay?"

"You told him *what*? No, Margaret, you can't stay here. Don't drag me into this."

"Why can't I go out to eat with him and then stay here? Your mom likes it when I show up."

"Teddy should pick you up at your house, not somewhere where you'd find an alley cat."

"I have never seen an alley cat at the park. You're not making any sense." Margaret regretted her tone as she spoke.

Little Teddy whimpered from Isabelle's bedroom.

"He can't reach the window ledge," Isabelle said. "But we can pick him up and hold him out here so he doesn't fall off. Margaret, don't be mad at me. I just don't want to be messed up with this Teddy stuff."

"I'll figure it out. I have to go now and think about it."

"Margaret, did you hear what I said? I don't want to be part of your drama and you know it."

"I can't say I'm going to meet him and then not show up. This is good practice for when I officially go out."

Isabelle stood. "Practice for what, deception?"

"Goodbye," said Margaret, a little sharply.

At the bottom of the steps that led to the front door, Miss Flora stood like a happy sentry.

"I just made a Boston cream pie and hoped that you and Isabelle would enjoy some of it with me," she said.

Everyone who knew Miss Flora knew that since her sister had died, she regularly had her dinner at one o'clock. This left her free to share dessert with anyone who wandered by, kind of like a Venus flytrap.

"My mom needs me," said Margaret. "She's very busy today." Would her entire life henceforth be based on lies? They came to her as easily as breath. "Maybe Isabelle and I could have some tomorrow, if there's any left."

Miss Flora laughed. She seemed to think that everything a person said was very amusing, unless it was about a dire tragedy, like a needle lost in the carpet or the Second World War.

"Of course you girls are welcome anytime, tomorrow or any day you like." She leaned toward Margaret and, in a conspiratorial whisper, said, "You know that I always have some dessert that is anticipating company."

"I know." How could Miss Flora's life be so happy when all she had to do was bake and waylay anyone with a stomach?

"Say hello to your parents and those adorable twins," said Miss Flora. "And your dear brother, too."

"I will."

13

Because it was Saturday, Mom made spaghetti and meatballs for dinner. Saturday evening was a prescribed program. While the dishes were being washed, Dad opened his shoeshine kit and sat at the kitchen table, polishing his dress shoes as well as Mark's in preparation for Sunday. Between dinner and *Gunsmoke* all the kids took a bath. When Margaret babysat or stayed overnight at Isabelle's house, she took her bath earlier in the day.

Now those simple rituals seemed precious.

At dinner Margaret ate a second helping and a small third one so that she wouldn't be hungry if she met Teddy. If she didn't eat much, she wouldn't be hungry later and wouldn't owe him gratitude or anything else; it wouldn't really be a date.

"Are you going to Isabelle's?" Mom asked. Could her mother see into her duplicitous mind? Why was she making this so easy?

"We're going to watch all the shows with Little Teddy," she said. Why did she identify Teddy as

"Little" to Mom? Mom didn't know about any other Teddy.

Mom wiped the stove top with the dishrag. "Margaret, you are so lucky to have had Grace for your friend for all these years—and then Isabelle, too."

Margaret continued to rinse and stack the plates. "I *am* lucky," she said.

"Why don't you ask Mark to take your turn with the dishes tonight so that you can go to Isabelle's as soon as you'd like?"

Mark was the only one left at the table, scraping the butterscotch pudding out of the bottom of the pan. Margaret turned to see the scowl on his face.

"I have a life, too," he said.

"No, you don't," said Margaret. "But you have pudding on your fat cheek."

"I'll wash the dishes only if you take my next two turns."

"Over my decomposed body," she said. "One turn."

Margaret wanted to leave even if only to go outside, where people wouldn't confuse her.

"Two turns," said Mark.

"Why do you two have to bicker so much?" Mom asked, drying her hands on her apron.

"We're just warming up," said Mark.

"One turn tomorrow and one turn next month," Margaret said.

Mom wore her sorrowful look, the one that reminded everyone that she had hoped for a harmonious family like the Cleavers of *Leave It to Beaver.*

It was a little too early to meet Teddy, but Margaret knew that this was her chance to exit.

"I'll see you after the shows," she said.

As she went out the front door, she realized that anyone looking out the living room window would see that she wasn't headed to Isabelle's. So she crossed the street and cut through Isabelle's backyard and walked down the alley to Thirty-Eighth Street and proceeded to the park, choosing to sit on a swing in front of the tennis court.

When Teddy drove up and parked on Bryant Avenue by the tennis court, Margaret knew that she still had a chance to end it all, whatever it was, before it began. But Teddy got out of the car and walked around to the passenger door, which he opened. Margaret stood up from the swing and walked toward the car as Teddy walked toward her. He'd changed his clothes—a fresh checked shirt with a collar, and khaki pants. She wore the T-shirt and pants that she'd worn when she was abducted earlier in the day, but she wasn't shoeless this time.

"Hungry?" Teddy asked.

Already this was difficult. If she said yes, she'd have to eat again. If she said no, what would they do?

"Sure."

"Bridgeman's okay?"

"Sure."

"Downtown or Lake Street?"

"Lake Street is closer."

"Lake Street, here we come," said Teddy.

In the car, Margaret couldn't think of anything to say as she stared at Teddy's right thigh. A few years earlier, the thighs of a boy at the lake cabin next door had intrigued Grace. Teddy's thigh looked more like a man's thigh, but she couldn't articulate the difference between a man thigh and a boy thigh. Mark had a thigh, as did their dad, but Teddy's thigh didn't look like either. Somehow it seemed to have more definition. Margaret wished that she could talk to Grace about this rather than being with Teddy.

Teddy set the radio dial to WDGY and turned up the volume. He turned to smile at her and said, "Okay?" Did he mean the radio station or being in his car? Neither was okay. She liked KDWB better, and she couldn't believe that she was forfeiting her life to be here.

"Okay," she said.

At Bridgeman's they sat in one of the last vacant booths, and each took a menu from behind the napkin holder.

"Do you like burgers?" asked Teddy. "I love the cheeseburgers better than anything."

The waitress appeared with a pad and pencil.

"Cheeseburger?" Teddy asked Margaret. "Or something else?"

"Cheeseburger."

"Two cheeseburgers," he said to the waitress. "And two chocolate malts." He looked at Margaret. "Is that okay?"

"Sure." Why did she say that? The thought of eating made her want to bolt, or worse.

"I went home and changed the oil this afternoon," Teddy said. "I like to do that a little ahead of the schedule in the manual."

Was this really happening—he was talking about his *car*? She would rather eat off the floor than hear about anything under a car hood. She couldn't be civil to someone who talked about his car on a date.

Margaret looked at the door and wondered if she had the nerve to stand up and leave. How could she trample on Grace's trust for this?

Teddy seemed to read her mind. "You probably don't care about cars, right?"

"No, I don't."

"I don't either, really. The car is my dad's, and I have to change the oil if I want driving privileges. It's just something I did this afternoon."

The combination of her guilt and his car talk made her doubt her sanity. If she stood up and caught a Lake Street bus going west, it would only be a twenty-minute ride and seven-block walk to her house. That was, if she had brought money. Margaret looked at the door and prayed that Teddy would vanish by the time she looked back. But she couldn't take her eyes off the door, because Daisy Winter was entering it with three friends. As Daisy and her friends scanned the restaurant for a seat, Daisy's eyes caught Margaret's. Daisy's curiosity won out; she whispered to her friends and approached.

"Hi, Margaret," she said, as she turned to look at Teddy. "Hi, Teddy."

Teddy stared at Daisy, who was wearing a ruffled rib-tickler top, even though it was too early in the season for an exposed navel.

"What are you up to?" she asked him.

"Taking the prettiest girl in town out for a bite to eat."

Daisy stared at Margaret as though she hadn't heard correctly. "Don't do anything I wouldn't do, Margaret," she said.

After Daisy returned to her group, Teddy leaned across the table. "Is she a friend of yours?"

"No. But she's in some of my classes. How do you know her?" Margaret asked. She cast another look at Daisy. Daisy was glorious until she spoke in her snippy voice and waved her hair like a windstorm.

"I used to go out with her sister."

"Her sister?"

"Right. Her sister is really nice."

Nice? When Daisy wasn't? Margaret's stomach—
full of spaghetti, meatballs, and lies—hurt badly.
She didn't care what she said to Teddy now. First
he talked about car oil and then admitted that he
had gone out with Daisy's sister. Maybe his other
girlfriends—at twenty years old, he must have had
dozens—listened to him talk about mufflers and tie-
rods because they were crazy about him.

"I started out on the wrong foot with you," Teddy
said. "Kidnapping, cars. Let's try again. What do you
do when you're not at school?"

"Homework."

Teddy laughed as though she had said something
funny.

"Okay. I spend a lot of time with Grace and Isabelle. Isabelle has a new puppy, so last night we
stayed overnight so we could watch the puppy be a
puppy."

"What's his name?"

His name. Now she would have to lie again. Or
would it be better to tell the truth so she didn't have
to be careful about not mentioning Little Teddy to
the original Teddy if she ever saw him again?

"He was that little dog that was across the street
when I picked you up this morning, right? He was
with your friend Isabelle. He looks like a terrier mix."

"Right."

"So, what's his name?"

"His name is Eddie."

"Eddie? Isabelle could add a *T* and he'd be my namesake."

"Then I'd never forget either of your names."

"Right."

The waitress appeared and poured the chocolate malts into glasses, leaving the excess malt in their respective tins. "The burgers will be out in a minute," she said.

"What do you do when you're not working or at school?" Margaret asked.

"I read a lot."

Margaret glanced at Daisy, who was staring at her, looking perplexed.

And here was Teddy, saying that he was a reader. Maybe everything would turn out perfectly after all. She imagined an evening when they would sit in front of one of the fireplaces at Hosmer Library, looking up from their respective books at each other, knowing that their lives would never be the same. But hovering beneath a library table was Grace, who loved Teddy with passion. Or maybe Grace was there to despise her, Margaret, who had stolen the man of her dreams.

"I just finished all of George Orwell for the third time, and I'm starting on Ray Bradbury again. I like so many authors, including Oscar Wilde. So many."

He looked at Margaret's plate. "Don't waste those fries," he said. "They're the best."

Teddy dropped Margaret off at the south end of Isabelle's alley, as requested. He gave her shoulder a squeeze when she thanked him for the meal. Although she felt as if she had just gone on a roller coaster after Thanksgiving dinner, Margaret managed to smile rather than throw up.

"Are we going to do this again?" asked Teddy.

Why did he have to ask her that right now? Of course she wanted to see him again, but she wanted a break until she could figure out what was happening.

"You look uncertain," Teddy said. "Maybe you'd feel better if I met your parents so you wouldn't have to sneak out."

"You're kind of old for me."

"I don't think of myself as elderly."

"My parents will be suspicious because you're in college."

"Should I drop out? Would that make things better?"

"You know exactly what I mean."

"I do?" Teddy's smile showed off his perfect teeth.

Behind the car, a little bell tinkled in the breeze. It was statistically impossible that Isabelle and Little Teddy would see them together, Margaret and big

Teddy, twice in one day. The puppy jumped at the passenger door and slid down.

"Hi, Isabelle," said Teddy, leaning over Margaret. "How's little Eddie this evening?"

Isabelle glared at Margaret. "Little Eddie is great."

"Glad to hear it." Teddy reached across Margaret to open the passenger door. "Margaret wants to walk home with you, I bet."

Margaret slid out, answering Teddy's goodbye without looking at him. Teddy drove away without making a production: no peeling tires, no U-turn in the middle of the street, no honking.

Little Teddy attempted to climb Margaret's leg as he whimpered with delight.

She felt like whimpering, too.

As Margaret walked down the alley with Isabelle, a little girl rode her tricycle, raising her hand in greeting as she passed. Her father walked next to her and smiled at Margaret and Isabelle.

When they were out of earshot, Margaret said, "Parents have no idea what they're getting into, do they?" As she said it, she wished she hadn't. "I'm sorry. You know what I mean."

"I know," said Isabelle. "I wish my dad was around so I'd know how he would have reacted to me now that I'm older."

"You've never done anything that he wouldn't have liked."

"I still have time. Now let's talk about Teddy, the guy. Do you want this to be happening?"

"I don't know."

"He seems to like you and Eddie."

"Very funny."

"Do you really, really like him?"

"I don't want to like him but I do."

"So the problem is?"

"Grace."

"Anything besides Grace?"

"No."

"Then tell Grace."

When Margaret didn't reply, Isabelle asked, "What did you talk about?"

"Everything but the pain in my stomach. Actually we talked about books. And Daisy Winter, who showed up at Bridgeman's with her friends. Teddy used to go out with her sister."

"You have to be kidding. How did it end?"

"I couldn't ask him."

"Will you ask him next time, for me?"

"I don't think I want to know."

"Okay. Let's get back to Grace. You have to tell her. And you have to tell your parents. It's hard to lie well. Something will trip you up."

"What have you ever lied about?"

"We're talking about you," Isabelle said. "What's the worst thing that can happen?"

"I'll have to sneak around. And never tell Grace."

"It's not worth it. Take a chance. Tell your parents. Tell Grace."

Margaret felt that Isabelle had planted a seed, or maybe the seed of a seed of a seed. Maybe, if she told her parents, her mother wouldn't purse her lips and her dad wouldn't look at her as if she were two years old and he couldn't understand what she wanted. Miracles happened. But then there was Grace.

Everyone was watching TV when Margaret entered the living room, so she sat down and watched the end of *Gunsmoke,* her resolve diminishing with every wise word uttered by Matt Dillon. When it was over, she said to Mom, "I need to talk to you and Dad." Her father had drifted into the kitchen before the credits and theme had stopped playing. "On the porch," Margaret said.

Mom went into the kitchen and said something to Dad, who reappeared with Mom and a glass of lemonade.

"Where are you guys going?" Mark asked. The twins stopped braiding each other's hair and looked up.

"Just talking," Mom said.

"Why do you need to talk on the porch?"

"Mark, you and the girls can finish picking up the sticks in the backyard."

"That's a ruse," said Mark.

"What's a ruse?" Karen asked.

"It's a trick to get rid of us."

"Will you give us a penny for each stick?" Kathleen asked Dad.

"It's getting dark out," Mark said. "Let's trip over sticks until one of us splits our head open."

Dad glared at Mark.

"I'm going, I'm going."

After Mom settled on the daybed and Dad sat in a lawn chair, Margaret shut the living room window that opened onto the porch and closed the door to the living room. She sat next to Mom. Maybe they thought she was failing all her classes. Why couldn't she have an uplifting surprise for them, maybe that she had won a trip to Costa Rica for her excellence in Spanish.

"I went out tonight with someone named Teddy that I met at the Emerald, where Grace works," she said. "He came over in his car this morning and asked me to go out tonight and I did. To Bridgeman's."

Mom looked at Dad with an expression that asked why Margaret was speaking in tongues.

"We thought you were with Isabelle," Dad said.

"Well, I was, later. For a little while."

"So it was a short date," said Dad. "Who is this fellow?"

Mom looked back and forth from Margaret to Dad as they spoke, as though following a tennis ball from racket to racket.

"We went out to eat and then he dropped me off, and I saw Isabelle and walked back with her." She didn't say that Isabelle was her designated conscience.

"Where did you meet this Teddy?" asked Dad.

"He's Grace's friend at work."

Dad looked at Mom, who didn't seem to have the words to address this crisis. "Would you like to introduce him to us?" he asked.

A rustling at the porch door caught everyone's attention. The top of a head—impossible to tell if it belonged to Kathleen or Karen—showed at the bottom of the window in the porch door.

"All done?" Dad called. Footsteps sounded as the twins ran.

Mom started breathing again. "You told us you were going to Isabelle's," she said. "I believed you."

"I know."

"Let's meet the young man," Dad said in a hearty voice. "What kind of car does he drive my daughter around in?"

"It's yellow."

"Four wheels and everything?"

"I guess so."

"Margaret, I am so disappointed that you lied to us," Mom said.

"I'm sorry." She hoped that Mom's lips would unpurse themselves and that she wouldn't start crying.

"I hope that you mean it."

"I do." Did she? If it hadn't been for Isabelle, could she have swallowed her guilt and forgotten it? Two things had not happened during this conclave, she realized. Her parents hadn't asked where Teddy went to school. They would assume that he was in high school, certainly not elementary school or college. Nor had they asked his age.

"Invite him over," Dad said.

"I will. He suggested it."

Mom's lips weren't pressed together quite as tightly.

This was the first hurdle. Next, Grace.

14

On Monday in the main hallway, between second and third periods, Daisy Winter planted herself in front of Margaret.

"Teddy, is it?" asked Daisy. "Teddy Alcott?"

Teddy *Alcott*? Margaret didn't know his last name.

"Yes, Teddy Alcott." Was this some kind of trap?

"He went out with my sister, you know," Daisy said.

"I know," said Margaret. Could Daisy see her heart thumping beneath her uniform blazer?

"He wasn't her type."

Sometimes a character's nose—or a horse's—"flared" in books that she'd read. But Margaret had never experienced it until she saw Daisy's nose flare as she spoke.

"My sister is particular about men," Daisy continued.

Margaret had never wanted to do anything as much as she wanted to kick Daisy—but where? In the shin? A swift, hard kick would be such a relief, even though she would be kicking her almost in front of the Virgin Mary statue that was crowned every May after the student body had processed to it in song.

Instead, Margaret said, "I don't care what you or your stupid sister think about anyone or anything."

"You witch." Framed by her cascading golden hair, Daisy's face was the color of an almost ripe tomato. The colors weren't complementary.

Margaret clamped her mouth shut to keep any words inside. She would not stoop to Daisy's level, whatever that was. Or had she already sunk? She had been in training her entire life to turn the other cheek. She was succeeding but only because it felt so delicious to flaunt her self-control. She glared at Daisy, who jerked around to leave, only to bang into an elfin freshman, who dropped her books on Daisy's foot.

"Watch where you're going, imbecile," Daisy yelled at the freshman.

Sister Loyola, the art teacher, who had been hurrying to her classroom, clutched Daisy by the arm and steered her toward the office.

Margaret proceeded to religion class, exhilarated with satisfaction over her controlled performance. She burned with the desire to tell Grace, which meant that she would have to tell Grace about Teddy in order for Daisy's rage to make any sense.

"Why do you look so happy?" Isabelle asked as she passed Margaret's desk en route to her own seat.

"I'll tell you on the way home, in great detail."

"Okay."

Teddy Alcott, just like Louisa May Alcott. Now she knew his last name. That was a good sign. The ability to enrage Daisy Winter was a good sign. She had simply walked down the main hall, something that she had done hundreds of times, and life went from normal to spectacular in a few packed seconds.

But why would anyone—including Daisy's sister—reject Teddy?

Margaret tugged herself away from that thought. She turned her sights to Isabelle's reaction to what had happened. Next she would figure out how to tell Grace everything.

15

Teddy called almost as soon as Margaret arrived home, and it felt as if he had been spying, perhaps following her in his car and then calling from the phone booth on the corner where the Thirty-Eighth Street bus waited before heading back east to the river.

"Hey, I just want to know if you told your parents about me or if you have to keep me hidden," he said.

"You were right," Margaret said. "They want to meet you."

"That's cool. Tonight?"

"I have a lot of homework because it's Monday. Maybe after school, later in the week."

"Thursday works. Then we'll be set for the weekend."

How can anyone have that kind of confidence? Margaret wondered. Would she assume that his parents would be besotted with her as well?

"I know when you're out of school," Teddy continued. "Just tell me which door you leave from."

Margaret thought back to the afternoon he had

driven by as she walked home with Isabelle and Francine. How did he know what time school ended? It was curious.

As dinner neared an end, Margaret mentioned the phone call, as if it was normal for her to have a twenty-year-old boy-man pick her up after school. But she couldn't hide Mark and the twins when Teddy came over, so they might as well know beforehand. Maybe they would settle down before Teddy showed up.

"That will be fine," Dad said.

"But, Harold, you won't be home from work when Margaret comes home with Teddy." Mom folded her napkin and placed it on the table.

"I'll be here," said Mark. "This guy must swing from a tree and have a tail if he wants anything to do with Margaret."

Margaret imagined grinding her shoe into Mark's foot but decided not to since she was having an adult conversation with her parents.

Kathleen and Karen put their spoons down, ignoring the pudding in the bottom of their bowls. "Who is that you're talking about?" Karen asked.

"Are you going to get married?" asked Kathleen.

"No one is getting married." Margaret worried about the twins' lack of tact. Were they like this away from home?

"Someone who lives here never will," Mark said.

Dad cleared his throat. "About work," he said. "I'll leave early." Although he didn't reprimand Mark, Margaret wondered whether Dad had ever imagined the kids he would be having dinner with every night of his life because he decided to marry Mom.

Margaret looked at her mother to see the shock register on her face. Dad never took sick or vacation time—except for the summer car trip when they stayed at campgrounds without plumbing—so that the pay would accrue and be available in case of death or disfigurement or another tragedy. Then Mom would have a buffer. Mom had given up her career plans after student teaching in a high school. She wouldn't say more than that it hadn't worked out.

"I'll be here," Mark said again.

Margaret resisted saying, "Where else would you be?"

"Well, that's settled," said Mom. "Thursday."

On the way home from school the next day, Margaret asked Isabelle, "Remember the day you walked to the river because you thought that Miss Dora had died during the night? And Grace and I found you in the rain. And you were really crying for your dad and your mom and yourself and everything that was so sad."

"Margaret, that's almost the craziest thing I've ever heard you say. How could I forget?"

"I know. I'm just trying to make an analogy."

"I can't imagine what it will be."

"I'm out in the rain, just not as much as you were. No comparison. But I need someone to rescue me, like Grace and I tried to rescue you."

"That's a terrible analogy. It's about Grace, isn't it?"

"Yes."

"Then we'll stop at her house on the way home," Isabelle said.

"But she'd rather come to your house because there aren't so many people and your mom is nice."

"No. We're going now."

"I don't need to tell her today."

Isabelle turned at the corner so that they were walking on Harriet Avenue. Central High School had an earlier release time, so Grace was at home. She was sitting on the front steps, holding a baby.

"Ten years, I had ten years without being responsible for a baby. Now this."

"Your mom wasn't expecting the last time I saw her," Margaret said.

"He belongs to my aunt, who's in the house. I hope my mom doesn't get any ideas."

"What's his name?" Isabelle asked.

"Andy."

Isabelle leaned down and rested her hand on the baby's cheek. "He's perfect," she said, her hand lingering. "Simply perfect." Reluctantly she straightened up. "Margaret needs to tell you something."

"Why can't she tell me that she needs to tell me something?"

"Grace, I went out with Teddy," said Margaret.

Grace snorted, which sounded like derision. "I know that you did. You could have told me earlier." The baby jerked in his sleep, and his fists curled even though his eyes didn't open. Grace handed the baby up to Isabelle, who put her arms out to receive him. "Go find his mother," Grace said.

Isabelle held the baby tightly as she walked to Grace's front door.

"Teddy told me that you went to Bridgeman's," Grace said to Margaret.

Margaret's heart slipped into her shoe. "Why didn't you tell me that you knew?"

"Why didn't you tell me that you were going out?"

"All we did was go to Bridgeman's. I had dinner before we went," said Margaret, knowing that her formerly full stomach would have no bearing on Grace's feelings.

Isabelle ran back to them, arms free. "Grace," she said. "She went in the car with Teddy to tell him to go away because she didn't want to go out with him and she didn't want her parents to see him, and he drove away with her kneeling in the passenger seat. I saw it."

"Why didn't you call and tell me about it after it happened?" Grace asked. No one answered.

"I don't even care about Teddy," Grace said to Margaret. "Not one iota. My magic didn't work on him. What matters is that you're into secrets."

"I wanted to tell you."

"Why didn't you?"

"Because she was afraid that she would hurt you," said Isabelle.

"Isabelle," Grace said, very slowly. "Isabelle, you are not the defense." She looked at Margaret. "I would never go out with someone to tell him that I would never go out with him, especially if my best friend would be upset, which I'm not."

"I promise you, Grace," said Margaret. "I promise that I will never keep anything from you again. I was wrong."

"I'm going inside now. I'm done with this crap," Grace continued, as she slowly stood. "Anyway, it wasn't about Teddy. It was about you committing a sin of omission. It's what you *didn't* say. That's what hurts the most." She stared at Margaret. "I *suppose* that *maybe* we can get past this at some time if you stop weeping all over the steps right now."

"Kiss and make up," Isabelle said, as Margaret put her head on Grace's shoulder and cried harder. Grace seemed to be carved out of granite. But her arm began to move stiffly, and she patted Margaret's back while her face remained stoical.

16

On Thursday Margaret was relieved that she didn't have to choose her clothes. Her school uniform was the only option, five days a week. Isabelle knew that Teddy was picking Margaret up after school, but she had refused a ride home. Margaret argued that Isabelle should accept the offer because Teddy would park within a few yards of Isabelle's front door. Isabelle countered that she would rather hear about it later, all of it, and that her presence might interrupt the natural flow of sparkling conversation between the couple.

A school day had never moved more slowly, even on the days when Margaret fell asleep in sixth-period religion and a fragment of her brain stayed on alert for detection. But twenty minutes after three o'clock in the afternoon arrived. Teddy had parked outside the side door per Margaret's insistence, because traffic always surged at the school's front and back. When he saw her, Teddy got out of the car and walked to the passenger side to open the door. Margaret pictured Mark, who would lock all the doors when he was first to the family's Ford Galaxy.

"Look at all the shrub lilacs," Teddy said. "It must be stunning when they're all in bloom."

Margaret hadn't noticed anything. "I don't usually come out this way," she said.

"Hey, I've never seen you in your professional outfit," he said. His freshly pressed shirt with a collar had a tiny plaid print that brought out the green in his eyes.

"I did dress up, just for you." She tried to keep her tone light. "Actually, I don't have a choice."

Teddy made a U-turn and then headed for Thirty-Eighth Street, which meant that neither Isabelle nor Francine nor anyone else would stare as the car passed.

"Are your parents predisposed to like me?" Teddy asked.

"I think so. If I'd said anything bad about you, they wouldn't care if they met you because they'd just tell me I couldn't see you."

"So the kidnapping was okay?"

"I forgot to tell them about that. Just Bridgeman's."

Teddy drove with care, slowing down at intersections where kids congregated on the corners. How could she have been so wrong about him in the beginning, imagining Teddy to be a swashbuckling, insensitive kind of boy-man? His fingernails were cleaner than hers and neatly trimmed. It wasn't his fault that a tiny bit of dark hair dusted his fingers between knuckle and hand. He was a thoughtful person who opened the passenger door for passengers and was probably burdened with the necessity of shaving twice daily.

Even as a marginally sneaky child, Margaret had never felt sick to her stomach as she neared the only home she had ever known. How would her parents see Teddy? As a kidnapper or the thoughtful older son they didn't have?

Teddy pulled up in front of the house, Margaret's door perfectly aligned with the strip of pavement on the boulevard. He smiled at her before opening his door and appearing on her side.

"Here we go," he said. "Salem witch trials. One of the first men accused."

"It will be worse than that," Margaret said, imagining some kind of showdown.

Dad was sitting in his recliner, casually rolling a cigarette.

"How do you do, Mr. Morris," Teddy said, extending his hand as Dad stood.

"It's good to meet you," said Dad. "Call me Hal."

Whose dad was this? Nobody under twenty-one called him by his first name.

"What did you drive Margaret home in?"

"An MG," Teddy said.

Dad walked the few steps to the window. "Morris Garage. Good little car."

"It's served me well, Hal."

"Those bumpers really reflect, don't they?"

"Nothing shines up like chrome."

Mom emerged from the kitchen with a plate of snickerdoodles. Her smile was so bright and unguarded that Margaret wondered if she would invite Teddy to dance. Instead, she suggested that everyone sit at the table. She called Mark and the twins, and they emerged like voles from the basement. Eyes crossed, Mark sat opposite Margaret, and the twins took turns whispering into each other's ears. Aside from these annoyances, Margaret thought that her family was acting appropriately.

Mom circled the table with a coffeepot.

"So what does your father do, Teddy?" asked Margaret's dad.

This was the embarrassing question he had asked his children's friends until Cecelia Archer, a neighbor girl whose father had abandoned the family when Cecelia was four years old, said, "I don't know." Later Mom told Dad that he had to stop asking. But here he was, at it again.

"He's a Minneapolis cop," said Teddy. "Twenty-two years."

Margaret imagined that she could read Mom's mind: "A police officer's son wouldn't dare get into trouble."

Dad asked Teddy a multitude of questions, but he seemed to coax them out of a willing Teddy rather than turning him inside out. Teddy was working toward a degree in mechanical engineering at the "U." He had an older sister who was a nurse, and a younger brother who played high school basketball. His mother and father met in the University of Minnesota Marching Band, in which his father played the tuba and his mother, the flute. For recreation, Teddy favored tennis in the summer and hockey during the winter.

Why hadn't she known these things about Teddy? Margaret wondered. She heard Grace's voice in her ear: "You have to *ask* him." What did they talk about? Books, a little. Cheeseburgers. How he didn't care to work on his car. What did they talk about on the phone? The events of their respective days.

Margaret's stomach began to calm as Teddy ate four more snickerdoodles and drank two glasses of milk. He seemed quite relaxed.

Mark stared as if he couldn't believe that Teddy was at the table because of Margaret.

"Could I ask you a question?" Mark finally said.

"Sure."

"You drive a stick shift, right?"

"Sure do."

"I thought that you'd drive a stick."

This seemed to embolden the twins, who whispered to each other. Then Karen asked, "What is your sister's name?"

"Holly," said Teddy. "She was born on Christmas Eve."

The twins looked at each other with approval. "That's a pretty name," Kathleen said, softly. "She's lucky that she has such a pretty name, for Christmas."

"I'm going to tell her that you said so."

The twins looked at each other with a deep sense of accomplishment.

"Do you have a student deferment?" Dad asked, and even the twins knew that he was referring to the war in Vietnam, which was on the news every night.

Margaret's stomach did a flip.

"Yes, Hal. I'm safe for now."

Dad said, "I thought so."

Mom got in a few questions as well, asking about his high school (Roosevelt) and his neighborhood (four blocks east of the Riverview Theater). In her eyes, it seemed, the imagined Teddy had transformed from a lecherous old man to young Teddy, the Eagle Scout that he was.

After Teddy left, saying that he needed to hit the

books after supper at home, Mom said to Dad, "He's such a gentleman."

"That he is," Dad said. "I'd pick him for my team."

Everyone seemed to have forgotten that he was a twenty-year-old who had plucked her, Margaret, out of a cafeteria downtown.

17

After dinner Margaret crossed the street to Isabelle's.

"They liked him?" Isabelle asked, as the girls sat in the living room. "Didn't they see how old he is?"

"Who?" asked Isabelle's mother, coming out of the kitchen.

"Margaret's boyfriend."

"You have a boyfriend, Margaret?"

"He's not my boyfriend," Margaret said. "We only went out one time."

"But he was at your house? Today?"

"Yes." How much should she say? "Isabelle said it was the right thing to do, to tell my parents."

"Good for you, Isabelle," said Isabelle's mother. "It's better to tell your parents than to go off and meet someone at the park." She winked at Margaret and moved toward the front door. "I have to see Miss Flora about something." Little Teddy followed her down the stairs.

"How does she know that I met Teddy at the park?"

"She doesn't. But she probably saw you walking down our alley toward the park and thinks that you did. I didn't tell her." Isabelle sighed. "But did Teddy perform nicely for your parents?"

"Nice? They'll want him to ask for my hand in matrimony so they can pull him into the family."

"They don't care how old he is?"

"Didn't seem to."

"Maybe he's acting," said Isabelle. "Maybe he's trying to get everyone to trust him and then he's going to kidnap you and take you to Las Vegas."

"He could have driven me to Las Vegas on Saturday. I'm more worried about Daisy. Why does she even care about Teddy and me unless Teddy dumped her sister?"

"There's something we're missing," Isabelle said.

"Not everybody who goes out with someone stays with that someone forever," said Margaret.

"Just like we're not best friends with everyone we ever met," Isabelle said.

"But Daisy's sister. We can't know that piece, but maybe she likes somebody better than Teddy."

"No," Isabelle said. "Teddy must have dumped her sister or Daisy wouldn't be so catty. We'll never know unless we have the facts. You'll have to get them from Teddy."

"I have to go home and sort this day out in my head."

"You can stay here and do that."

"I want to. But I want to go home and be alone."

"You're never alone there," said Isabelle.

"You're right."

"Let's sit on the porch for just a little while. Stay for supper. On the porch," Isabelle said.

Mark was sitting on the edge of the couch watching TV when Margaret walked into the living room. He looked as though he was eagerly awaiting a train.

"Do you really think he'll give me a ride?" he asked. "Can I call him?"

Could she resent him for liking Teddy?

"Maybe after I've gone out with him a little more. A week or two weeks or something."

"Really, Margaret?"

Her name sounded funny when he said it, maybe because he wasn't yelling it or being sarcastic.

"Sure."

Mark grinned, looking almost demented. "It's like having a really cool big brother."

Margaret thought of saying that if he had a big brother, the big brother would find him pesky, just as his big sister did. But she felt so grateful, so adored, that she bestowed a smile on him, her brother, a boy who believed that she had brought a wonderful gift for the whole family to enjoy. Who knew?

Before she fell asleep, Margaret pored over

recent events. Mom and Dad liked Teddy. They had life experience, so Teddy must be okay according to the standards of the 1930s or whenever they learned about grown-up rules. Besides, at age twenty, Teddy couldn't be smart enough to completely fool parents who were more than twice his age and suspicious, could he? Mark liked Teddy, too, and the twins had probably designed their flower girl dresses already. She, Margaret, had worried, but that was her nature. Or maybe she expected the worst of everyone— Teddy, her parents, the kids. At least she didn't worry in her sleep, or did she?

18

In Spanish class, Señorita Waters seemed to have love—or at least quinceañeras—on her mind, along with a hickey on her neck.

"In many Spanish-speaking countries, in an earlier time, girls were celebrated at age fifteen—the desired age for marriage." Señorita seemed to have lost her fluency in Spanish as she tried to avoid looking at Marguerite Steel, who was staring at her with intensity. "If they weren't married by fifteen, the only recourse was the convent. The parties were lavish."

"¿Qué es?" Marguerite inquired, pointing at Señorita's neck.

Señorita Waters must have known that her hickey was visible; it peeked out from under her collar. "Bug bite," she said, in English.

"¿Qué?" asked Marguerite.

"A bug bite."

Daisy let out an exaggerated guffaw, which a few of the girls supported with snickers. Everyone knew that Señorita Waters was engaged to Jorge Martínez, who had been an archaeologist at the Teotihuacan pyramids in Mexico before he followed Señorita and took a job at the University of Minnesota.

Everyone knew what a hickey was because some of the girls showed up with them, usually after a weekend. Marguerite was a naive girl who spent much of her weekend practicing on the pipe organ at her parish church.

Margaret tried to imagine how Teddy might give her a hickey. Would he nuzzle her face and inch down to her neck? Or go straight for the neck like a vampire? The only part of her that he had touched was her shoulder. He didn't seem like the kind of person who would wrestle her to the ground but more like a boy-man who would say, "May I kiss you good-night?" and then bend toward her without touching anything but her lips.

"¿Cuántos años tiene?" asked Señorita. How old are you? Margaret looked up and saw that she was being addressed.

"Diecisiete, Profesora." Seventeen.

Señorita continued: "¿Te vas a casar pronto?" Will you marry soon?

"Después de Ud., Profesora." After you do, Professor.

Even Señorita Waters laughed.

"Silencio, por favor," Señorita said to Daisy, who continued to laugh over a private joke with the girl across the aisle from her. Margaret turned slightly in order to see Daisy and, for the first time, thought that she had never seen Daisy smile, even when she was laughing; maybe there was glee but no joy. She wished that she could say in Spanish, "Your smile isn't a smile but bile." It wouldn't rhyme, but the sentiment would translate.

When class was over, Señorita stopped Margaret at the door and stepped aside with her. "Margaret," she said, "it is such a gift to be funny in a second language. It goes beyond words."

"Thank you," Margaret said, because here was yet another occasion when she didn't know if this was supposed to be the beginning or the end of a conversation. She smiled at Señorita, even though she wanted to move her eyes down to get a better look at her "bug bite."

Teddy called to talk on the phone almost every other evening. He was easy to talk to because he asked Margaret questions about her day. On Wednesday he asked her to go to a dance at Coffman Union at the "U," where one of his favorite bands would be playing.

"I said I'd go," Margaret said to Isabelle that evening. "But I'll feel so stupid because I'm so—I don't know."

"You're what? Too young? You're not going

to wear a high school letter jacket or something. Nobody cares."

As she could have guessed, Teddy was a fabulous dancer. During the slow dances, he didn't drape himself over her but rather kept a respectful distance between them. The dim lighting, the loud music, the din of voices, Teddy's hand on her shoulder between dances—it was a parallel universe that nothing could seep in to disrupt. At one point, the most delicious moment of her life, Teddy stood behind her with his arms encircling her waist and his chin resting on her head. Life would never improve after that moment, she knew.

On the way out, just before they entered the brightly lit hall, Teddy leaned down and whispered, "You are perfect." She couldn't reply because her heart was in her throat and it was choking her.

If he had asked her to go out to eat, she would have despaired. Sitting in Bridgeman's or anywhere where silverware rattled and plates were slammed down on tables and unfortunate people who were not her had meaningless conversations—no, that could not be tolerated. But Teddy drove to Lake Harriet and pulled into a parking lot. He put his arm around Margaret and gently nudged her closer.

"It's beautiful here, isn't it?" he said, his eyes on the moon.

What could she say? "I never imagined that one night could be better than every other night of my life." "I never knew how it feels to have happiness circulating in my blood." "How could heaven be better than this?"

"Yes," she said. "It's more beautiful than any moon I've ever seen." That wasn't true, she thought, because it's always the same moon. But Teddy must know that she wasn't that stupid.

"I agree."

They continued to stare at the moon.

"I could stay here with you all night," Teddy said, putting his hand on the back of her neck.

"Me, too. I mean with you."

"But your parents might not have a good opinion of me if we did."

Who cared about her parents?

Teddy turned the key in the ignition.

What was the hurry? The moon wasn't going anywhere, was it?

Teddy hummed "Blue Moon" on the way home. He opened the passenger-side door when he parked in front of Margaret's house. At the front door, he held her face in his hands and brushed her lips with his so lightly that it felt like contact with a breeze.

"See you, soon," Teddy said as he turned toward the steps, before Margaret had thought of saying, "Thank you."

On Sunday afternoon at Isabelle's, Margaret told Grace and Isabelle everything that had happened with Teddy.

"Oh, the moon!" Grace said. "Teddy, Teddy, I never knew the moon was so big! I think the moon that hangs over Minneapolis is the largest in the world!"

Isabelle tried to stifle her laughter. Seated on the floor, she turned away, but Margaret could see her body shake. She couldn't be angry with either Grace or Isabelle because she needed them.

"Please, Teddy, don't allow the butterfly that brushed my lips to attack me again!" Grace was enjoying her monologue tremendously. "My mother might see the imprint of a wing on my chaste mouth!"

Still turned from Margaret, Isabelle shook with her head lowered almost to her lap, and Margaret acknowledged to herself that this was a physical feat, even as she hoped that someday Isabelle would be serious again.

Little Teddy jumped on Isabelle's back and barked, which only made Isabelle laugh harder.

Grace continued to revel in her monologue. "On our next outing, dear Margaret, my moon girl, we shall bring Little Teddy along, and he shall sit between us, and we will share the brushing of lips with him as well."

Margaret picked up a *Seventeen* magazine and

flipped through it, hoping that Grace and Isabelle would burn out if she ignored them.

Isabelle rolled onto her back and wiped her eyes with the neck of her T-shirt.

"Grace, stop," she said as she continued to shake. "Margaret wants to talk."

"About what?" Grace asked, pulling a sober face. "Going out with someone who can't keep his eyes off the moon?"

"Margaret, really, it's not a big deal," Isabelle said. She avoided eye contact with Grace as she pulled herself up. "He's just nice, and he doesn't want to maul you."

"Right," Grace said. "Your parents would notice if he chewed your lips off."

Margaret didn't say anything. If she were quiet, maybe Grace would be serious.

"I remain confounded," said Grace, furrowing her forehead as if trying to find an answer behind it. "Maybe he doesn't want to scare you, an innocent schoolgirl who lives in the bosom of her wary guardians."

"Maybe it is the reason," Isabelle said, as Grace snorted. "Look at Margaret. She's so nice and innocent. And she's pretty. He doesn't want to make her rush."

"I'd like to rush a little bit," said Margaret.

No one commented.

"Grace," Isabelle asked, "if every man wanted to marry the nicest and prettiest woman in the world, why would so many men marry women who are plain and kind of boring?"

"Or like my mother," said Grace.

"Your mother must have something going for her," Isabelle said, although she couldn't imagine what it was.

"Chemistry, that's it," Grace replied. "You like somebody's smile or their shape, and before you know it, you have a framed wedding photo in the living room and a litter of kids."

"Margaret, don't worry about Teddy," said Isabelle. "He likes you enough to meet your family. He doesn't want to show how much his chemistry likes your chemistry yet."

Chemistry. The reaction of matter in science. Margaret didn't want to think about it right now. She simply wanted to know if Teddy had ever wanted to combust with joy as she did.

19

As spring transformed into summer, Margaret and Teddy continued to see each other on Saturday nights—dinner, movies, walks. At Lake Harriet on an unusually warm evening just after Memorial Day, Margaret decided to buy Teddy a treat at the pavilion.

"Wait here," she said. "I'll be back."

Teddy made a long face as he sat on a bench under a large elm. "Don't forget me, Margaret," he said. "I'll always be here, unless you elope with someone in the next ten minutes."

The line for drinks was long, and Margaret prided herself on choosing the ice cream line, which had no one in it. With a chocolate cone in each hand, she returned to where she had left Teddy, but Teddy wasn't there. She walked farther, but the next spot that looked identical to the original one now harbored a family with a standard poodle with a sharp bark. By the time Margaret found Teddy, the ice cream had melted and soaked through the wads of napkins that she had wrapped around the cones.

It had dripped onto her white sundress with the square neck and red rickrack at the bottom of the skirt. Teddy stood when he saw her coming, and he threw his head back and roared with laughter as she came closer. When she stood in front of him, ice cream dripping down her inner arms as she held the cones up, Teddy stood in front of her and encircled her neck with his arms.

"Your shirt," Margaret said. "Your beautiful, clean shirt." She pulled back and stared at the damage on both fronts. Teddy pulled her back, so close that she couldn't tell if his heart or hers was beating so fiercely.

"Now everyone will know that we're a couple," he said. "We send our clothes to the same laundry."

"I don't believe it," she said.

"What don't you believe?"

"What you just did."

"Is there a better option?" asked Teddy. "Cry or make a joke? You know that I'm washable."

Margaret wanted to say the three little words to him. How could she ever love anyone as much as she loved him at this moment?

"It's not as if I'm going to a job interview tonight," he said.

Margaret took the few steps to the trash can, into which she tossed the soggy cones. "My hands are so sticky," she said.

"We can take care of that later," he said. He gestured for Margaret to sit next to him on the bench, and he sat down and took hold of one of her hands. "Now everyone can see that we're stuck on each other."

Margaret laughed so hard that the walkers on the path in front of them turned to look. Never had anyone in the world been luckier, ever. Margaret looked at the boy-man that she wanted to be with for the rest of her life, and he looked back at her with mirth—all for me, Margaret thought. Mirth. In the bandstand, the Minnesota Pops began to play "June Is Bustin' Out All Over," and Margaret knew the sentiment.

School was out on June 10. Margaret spent the last day of English class watching Brian Briar, son of the school secretary, as he mowed the lawn. What if Teddy had a job like that, a job where he was visible to her even as he made money to take her out?

She could not stop thinking about Teddy. He was perfect. Yes. And no. He was the kind of perfect that parents who weren't his parents could love, as did all the waitresses and ticket takers they encountered, and all the employees at the Emerald, so Grace said. She loved him, in all his perfection, without reservation. Except that his perfection was sometimes a bit frustrating.

Even so, Margaret wanted to throw her arms

around him and scoop him—body and soul—into her life, without reservations.

At Lake Harriet, on the first Saturday after school was out, Teddy asked Margaret if she was ready to go in the water.

"Let's wait," she said. Only a handful of kids were in the water—although the dock had lured some teenagers—and little kids were running to the water's edge, giggling when the water flowed over their ankles. Teddy scooped Margaret up from the warm sand and ran into the water. Typically a non-screamer, Margaret shrieked as the water splashed upward. Don't drop me, that's what she wanted to cry out. She wanted to be kept close to Teddy's very manly and moderately hairy chest, even as her ribs hurt from being held so tightly. She wanted Teddy to press her to his chest and kiss her until she didn't know if she was drowning in water or love.

Teddy threw her into five feet of water, between the ropes and the dock.

Long ago, when she was only twelve, Sherman Jensen had playfully—although it hadn't seemed that way at the time—pulled her off the ladder to the dock. Underwater, she hadn't known if she was scrambling up, down, or sideways. But much later, she realized that Sherman had wanted to touch her and that this was the only way he knew how to do it.

Teddy seemed to touch her because it was a requirement.

Now he began to swim to the same dock where Sherman had tried to get her attention. She followed, swimming more slowly than Teddy because she had not mastered the skill of dipping her face in the water like Olympic swimmers and others. Looking ahead, she saw something that she knew but had never acknowledged: everyone on the dock looked as if they were in junior high, with the exception of a handful of high school kids. Why hadn't she noticed this before? Was it because she and Grace and Isabelle rarely went to the dock anymore? Maybe it was different at the lake where Teddy swam when he wasn't with her.

Teddy was climbing the ladder. Teddy sometimes swam with her, but more often he swam ahead. Was water another place where he could separate without being conspicuous?

He loved her. He was attentive and happy. Wasn't he?

Dad wasn't exactly trailing Mom every day or watching TV with both arms around her waist or kissing her passionately when he came home from work.

Margaret thought of other couples on the beach that she didn't want to think about. They rubbed tanning lotion on each other's bodies as slowly as if they were trying to reach the unseen layers of the epidermis; they shared sodas, they nuzzled, they curled up like puppies.

When Teddy had a chance to snuggle, he wriggled away.

He played Monopoly with the twins.

He talked baseball with Dad.

He asked Mom about the family in which she'd grown up.

He drove Mark around the lake in the MG.

He did not love her. He was waiting for someone better to come along. He was killing time.

"I saved a place for you, Margaret," he said, as Margaret put her foot on a rung of the ladder. There he was, a sardine on the dock with younger sardines that jostled each other with exuberance.

Teddy did a backflip off the side of the dock, quickly enough to climb the ladder only one person behind Margaret.

"Don't try to beat that, my perfect flip and recovery. It's my specialty."

"I know."

Teddy squeezed her shoulder, and Margaret wondered at how robotic a hand could feel.

"You okay?" he asked.

Before Sherman Jensen moved away, he and Margaret had kissed in the park. The last time they were together there, rain began to pelt them, so they tucked themselves under the eaves of the Theodore Wirth House, which they had believed was haunted when they were little kids. Nothing could have separated them expect for a bat in her hair or fear of her mother, if her mother had known they were outside in a lightning storm in a park with a trillion trees.

She didn't think about Sherman very much because that was light-years ago. But as Teddy cannonballed off the dock again, she knew that she was seeing something that she didn't want to understand or acknowledge: Teddy wanted to be with her, but he didn't want to be with her.

"I'm going to swim out while the lifeguards are changing shifts," he called. He waved, but Margaret didn't wave back. Teddy would return, and they would sit on the blanket that he always had in the car trunk, and they would talk about what they were reading, and he would bring her home and go to his late shift at the Emerald.

When it was time for Teddy to leave, he stood and put out his hand for Margaret to grasp and be pulled up.

"I'm going to stay for a while," she said.

"How will you get home?"

"The same way I did before I knew you. I'll walk."

"Sure?" he asked.

"Sure." Even as she said it, she wanted to get into his little car and ride home, simply because it was exhilarating to be with Teddy even when confusing thoughts swirled around her head. By the time she had changed her mind, Teddy was almost to the car.

Margaret lay on her back and tried not to think about anything except how interesting it was that the sun took a personal interest in her, its warmth making each pore feel alive and sleepy at the same time.

In spite of the noise that surrounded her, she fell asleep until a sandstorm woke her.

"We saw lover boy taking off," said Grace, as she stood above Margaret, trickling sand on Margaret's stomach.

Grace seemed to not care about Teddy anymore, but Margaret felt a sliver of discomfort whenever Teddy came up in conversation.

"He's not my type," Grace proclaimed occasionally. "He's a Boy Scout poster, someone who has his knot-tying badges framed."

Grace had achieved her three goals: held on to her job at the Emerald, acquired a slightly hoodlumish boyfriend named Lonnie, and scored her driver's license, although the car that her uncle gave her for fifteen dollars was usually jacked up in Lonnie's backyard.

Isabelle hadn't been as successful, based on Grace's criteria, but Margaret knew that with Little Teddy in her life, Isabelle was probably happier than Grace. Margaret did not care too much about a job or a car, because Teddy more than made up for them.

20

The summer before senior year continued to unfold lazily. No homework, more time for reading. No job, more babysitting. No car, more time to walk to the lake with Isabelle or Grace or both of them. More time to watch *Mel's Matinee Movie* at one o'clock.

Teddy fit in neatly. Saturday night and one weekday afternoon. Grace saw Teddy more than Margaret did because of their jobs at the Emerald.

"Does Teddy flirt with other people?" Margaret asked Grace as they sat on the sand at the main beach at Lake Harriet.

She had meant "girls," not people, but she didn't need to clarify for Grace.

"He's kind of the same with everyone, happy face and kidding. Really, Margaret, even I—who understand human nature so well—think that he doesn't care who he talks to, and that includes old people."

"That means that he's nice, Grace," said Isabelle.

"Okay. You need an example." Grace leaned to reapply suntan lotion to her legs. "Here's an example. Hector is this really old, scary cook. He's about eight feet tall and glares at the staff as if we're too stupid to know the difference between his pot roast and pork chops."

Margaret stared at Grace's hair, strands of strawberry and blond that mingled and changed with the sunlight. Isabelle's light-brown hair waved gently, which made Margaret consider that she might stop ironing her own hair for the summer because the humidity always riled it up no matter how much she worked on it.

"Anyway," Grace continued, "there's a server named Nancy Wright, who can barely button her uniform over her chest. So does she go up a size? No, she leaves the top button unbuttoned as if she needs to do that in order to breathe. Hector makes mashed potatoes every day that Nancy works so that he can watch Nancy lean over not only to scoop potatoes but to add gravy, too."

"What a yucky guy," Isabelle said.

"Other guys, ones who are closer to Nancy's age, aren't so obvious. But they hang around her like puppies. Nancy really likes Teddy because he treats her like a person, not a vixen posing as a cafeteria worker."

Grace looked at Margaret. "Don't worry," she said. "Teddy isn't looking. And he talks about you all the time. 'My girlfriend, Margaret, and I went to see *The Sand Pebbles,* and after that we went canoeing at

Cedar Lake, and then we saw another movie while we were canoeing and had popcorn and looked at the biggest moon ever until we went to another movie.'"

Isabelle held her stomach as she laughed. Margaret knew that she would have been laughing if Grace's mimicry hadn't been based on Teddy.

"We haven't had a Lonnie report lately," Margaret said to Grace, as Isabelle's laughter dwindled to deep breaths.

"He may be history soon. He's convenient, but I'd like to do more than make out in his stupid car with the lumpy seats. I don't mean *more,* I mean *go* someplace." She looked at Margaret. "If we switched boyfriends once in a while, you'd get pawed occasionally, and I'd get something to eat."

Margaret imagined a better version. Teddy would pick her up, then wait for Isabelle to sail out, and, lastly, stop for Grace, who would hop in the back seat. They would all go to the Riverview, where Teddy would buy popcorn for everyone and drive everyone home and kiss her, Margaret, seriously in the car before walking to the front door and kissing her more seriously before reluctantly leaving. That would be satisfaction.

21

After the movie on Saturday, as Teddy headed toward Lake Street, Margaret said, "Let's go to a lake instead of Bridgeman's."

"Really? You're not hungry?"

"I had a tub of popcorn. I'm not hungry."

"But you're always hungry, even after the tub."

"I said, I'm not hungry." She was never hungry after the buttery popcorn. She ate at Bridgeman's because it was a shared activity.

"Margaret, you're shaking things up," he said, in his good-natured way. "Okay, let's go to Lake Nokomis for a change. We never go there."

"I've never been there." It wasn't on her radar, even though it was probably only a few miles from home. Without a car, she lived in a small town with its own stores, her own school and church, her own lake. There was downtown, but the number four bus came by every few minutes and made it an easy outing. Teddy was expanding her world. Lake Nokomis.

At the lake they sat on a bench and looked at the gauzy moon, and Margaret knew that if she had been born a few centuries earlier, she would have wondered what held the moon up in the sky. She still wondered, but she knew there was an answer.

"What are you thinking about?" she asked Teddy.

"There's another full moon to look at, with you."

There it was, in a nutshell. The moon made him happy. I'm happy that the moon makes him happy, she thought. And I'm an added feature? Why did she have to ruin this time by being jealous of the moon. It wasn't the moon's fault that she couldn't compete with it. "She walks in beauty, like the night / Of cloudless climes and starry skies," according to Lord Byron, a dead poet. Would Teddy choose her as the star of a poem, or would he choose the starry nights?

"Let's sit on the grass," she said.

"Why?"

"It's natural."

"The wood on this bench is natural," Teddy said.

"But it's covered with some goop to protect it from the elements." Margaret knew that he wanted to protect his khakis. Could they have reached an old, familiar stage without having passed through a passionate one? "Will you take me home now?" she said.

Teddy put his arm around her shoulder. "Margaret, Margaret, Margaret," he said.

"Margaret," she said to him. Was she channeling

Grace again? She wondered if she had any quality that Grace channeled.

"I'm tired," she said. "I'd like to go home."

"Stay here," Teddy said. "I'll be back in two minutes."

She sat on the bench and waited, counting the seconds. If he didn't return in three minutes, she would stand and walk home. She could find her way easily except that some north–south streets didn't go through because of Minnehaha Creek.

Teddy ran to the bench, holding a blanket. With a flourish he shook it and laid it on the grass.

They lay side by side on the scratchy wool, Teddy entranced with the moon. Margaret propped herself up on one elbow and stared at Teddy's beautiful face: green eyes glistening in the moonlight, Roman nose, strong jaw. She leaned over him, placing her head on his chest. As long as she could remember, teachers, priests, and her grandmother had promoted the glory of heaven as the ultimate and everlasting reward. But with her head on Teddy's chest, she couldn't believe that she could be suffused with more joy if St. Peter held a Dairy Queen Buster Bar and a puppy for her at the pearly gates of heaven. In spite of having to compete with the moon, she felt the thrill of contact with the wide chest that supported her head.

Teddy reached for her hand and held it.

Margaret wanted more than anything to experience one passionate kiss in her life, and she wanted it to be with Teddy. But she couldn't say, "I want a passionate kiss." It wasn't like ordering a cheeseburger.

She lifted her head in order to look into his eyes, which were shut. Was she invisible? She leaned over him, listened to him breathing in and out, and kissed his cheek. When there was no response she kissed his lips, which felt like pencil erasers.

Was there such a thing as deep, passionate chaste love?

With a start, she felt Teddy's arms encircle her as he flipped her from her side to her back and leaned over her, covering her mouth so completely that she couldn't breathe because Teddy's face smashed her nose. When she pounded on his back, he stopped for air and, with incomprehension, stared at her. Somehow Margaret knew that he wasn't kissing her but someone that she couldn't see.

Teddy composed his face. "I'm so sorry, Margaret," he said.

"Why?"

"For what I just did."

Questions hovered, closer than the crickets' familiar music.

"Do you want to go home now?" asked Teddy.

How could she answer? No, I don't want to go home. I don't want to go home until I know why you looked like you'd seen a ghost when you opened your eyes.

"Margaret, you're special," Teddy said as he sat up on the blanket.

She didn't know how to reply.

"You are so nice to me," he said.

The most benign word in the world.

"But I'm not like that."

Like what?

"I'm not like a lot of guys."

No, you're better.

"I'd like to keep going out with you."

You make it sound as if we're renewing a contract.

Margaret swelled with what Teddy wasn't saying.

"I'm a queer man."

Queer was one of her mother's all-purpose words. "This is a queer turn of events." "How queer that the twins didn't finish their corn before they left." "It's queer that I forgot to put a stamp on that letter."

"I like men," Teddy said.

Margaret waited. Who didn't like men, if they weren't old?

"There's a chance I'll get over it."

Over it? Over what? Her brain rummaged, straining to understand something that had no context.

"You probably don't know any queers," Teddy said, without looking at Margaret.

She didn't want him to talk anymore because she

didn't want to think about what he was saying. She wanted to go home.

"Margaret, I'm a homosexual."

She had never known that a person could black out while sitting upright. After the inside of her head went dark, she came back. She began to cry.

Oscar Wilde. They had talked about his books at Bridgeman's. Or was it only Teddy who talked about him? Margaret had seen *The Importance of Being Earnest* on stage at a public high school, and they had both read *The Picture of Dorian Gray*. Oscar Wilde had gone to prison for—what?—doing something with a man. Margaret had not understood that it was more than friendship, although she had wondered what they had done together to put Oscar in the clinker.

This was why Daisy had said that Teddy wasn't her sister's type.

"I hope that we can still be friends," Teddy said, his hand covering hers.

"Why?" Margaret asked. "Why don't you change?" She began to cry again, although she could not have sorted out whom it was for: Teddy trapped in an alien body or herself, because Teddy wouldn't ever be her boyfriend, but he had pretended that was what he wanted.

"It seems that's the way I am." He looked as if he was in pain but couldn't locate the source. "Can you do one thing for me? Please don't tell Grace and Isabelle."

Margaret gently removed her hand from beneath his. "Not telling" wasn't "one thing." He was asking for a blanket of silence, forever. She wondered if she could understand what Teddy was talking about without telling Grace and Isabelle.

Teddy had used her as a cover, a girlfriend.

"Why me?" she asked. What if other people knew, what if *Daisy Winter* knew? Margaret felt like a freak. How could she not have seen?

In the moonlight, Margaret looked at Teddy's face. He looked unmasked. He didn't answer.

Teachers and other grown-ups thought that Margaret was a nice girl, a very good and nice girl. But that came easily to her because she hated conflict. She had never researched the inside of her head to find out why she was so acquiescent. What would it be like to be nice to someone—or try to understand him—without putting herself into the equation? That didn't feel possible. She began to cry again, even though she wasn't sure if it was mostly for herself and a little bit for Teddy or possibly the other way around.

Margaret put one arm around Teddy's middle and then the other. He put his head on her shoulder and began to sob. They held each other, crying, for a long time, until Teddy finally stood up and put his hand out for Margaret.

22

Margaret's mother sat in the big chair next to the living room window, so that Margaret and Teddy saw her silhouette when they pulled up in front of the house. The porch light was the only one on in the still neighborhood.

"What will you tell her?" Teddy asked. It was twenty minutes past three o'clock in the morning, and the first time that Margaret had heard hesitancy in Teddy's voice.

"I don't know. I could tell her that it's the first time I slept with someone, but she might take that the wrong way."

"We were actually sleeping, but you have to choose your words carefully," Teddy said. "I should go in with you and explain."

"No. Nothing you say will make any difference, because I'm the one who's her kid."

Teddy didn't walk her to the door and butterfly kiss her. But he said something he had never said earlier, "I love you, Margaret."

This was fear and sorrow speaking, Margaret knew.

"I love you, too," she said. It came out of her mouth like a breath she had been holding. It was easier to say than she had imagined, but she knew that it meant she was sorry. She was sorry that he didn't love her the way she had wanted.

The porch door and inside door were unlocked. Mom didn't need to say a word in order to radiate her displeasure and disappointment.

"I know what you're thinking," Margaret said. "I'll tell you where I was."

Mom sat stiffly, and Margaret pulled Dad's hassock away from his chair and sat on it. Tonight—which was now morning—had been so sad that she couldn't lie, because she wanted her mother to know how sad life could be.

"Teddy and I went to Lake Nokomis and fell asleep on a blanket." She might as well have said that she was pregnant.

Mom didn't seem to know what to say, probably because she didn't want to know any details.

"It isn't what you think," Margaret said. "Teddy isn't like that." It felt so easy, telling the truth. "Teddy is queer."

Mom looked confused. "I feel queer sometimes, everyone does, but that's no excuse to stay out until after three o'clock in the morning."

Margaret realized that she was taking pleasure in this conversation.

"No, he's *queer*."

"Margaret, that's not an excuse for his behavior. Your father and I trusted Teddy."

"That's because he is trustworthy. But he's queer, he told me."

Mom's expression changed from disapproval to confusion.

"Queer," said Margaret. "He has feelings for guys more than girls. I was his cover."

Mom looked as if she was choking on an explosion of emotions.

"Oh, Teddy," she said, with a little cry. "Our dear Teddy." Tears began to run down her face, and she dabbed at them with the sleeve of her lilac print summer nightgown. "Poor, dear Teddy. It will be so difficult. My Uncle Porter, he was that way. He was married, but there were rumors. We called him 'funny, our funny uncle.'"

Margaret hadn't known Uncle Porter. He had moved to Florida with a florist before she was born. She didn't know that Mom knew how to use the word that way, "funny."

"What should we do?" Mom asked. "Teddy should know that we care about him."

Whose boyfriend was this?

"I don't think you have to do anything," said Margaret.

"But he should know that we love him."

"Why aren't you concerned about me?"

"You'll be fine, Margaret. You have years ahead of you to have boyfriends. Teddy will have a lifetime of trials."

Who was this woman? The patron saint of "funny people"?

"You've taken my issue away from me," Margaret said.

"It is not your issue, Margaret. It's Teddy's issue, and you know that." She rose and kissed Margaret on the forehead. "Poor, dear Teddy."

"Are you going to tell Dad?"

"I'm not sure. But he'll have to know why Teddy isn't around anymore."

"Maybe you could tell him that most seventeen-year-olds don't stay with their first boyfriend forever." Maybe Dad didn't need to know. He seemed to be a regular man, and maybe he hadn't had an Uncle Porter.

"Good night," said Margaret.

"Good night."

In bed Margaret tried to sort out her feelings. Since knowing Teddy, she had floated above Earth's surface. But some days, a bubble with questions inside hovered overhead. Tonight was betrayal.

What was Teddy thinking about? He didn't intend to hurt her. What had it been like for him to go out with Daisy Winter's sister? She probably rode around in Teddy's MG with her clothes off, and

Teddy didn't notice. Who knows what she had told Daisy?

Teddy probably pretended he was a macho guy when he was with macho guys. But did he ever slip? He didn't look at Nancy's cleavage at the Emerald, and he had been noticed because of it.

Had she, Margaret, ever known Teddy? At first she had been sneaky as she figured out what to do. Then she'd spent a lot of time trying to understand why he was a shoulder squeezer instead of a smoocher. Now she felt sad for him because he had to navigate the world with caution.

She heard the twins breathing on the other side of the upstairs. Life was so simple for children. No, it wasn't. She thought of Sherman and how she grew to love him after a bumpy beginning. And then he left, not because he wanted to but because he had to move with his parents. Maybe everyone's life got harder, like Mom's life: getting up at twenty minutes past six every morning when the alarm blasted. Why at that exact time? Did Mom feel that she was sleeping in by setting the alarm five minutes after six fifteen? Someday she would ask her how she could have ever been happy when she had to get up in the dark much of the year to serve breakfast to four somewhat ungrateful children and a fairly nice husband.

Margaret fell asleep. The wondering was overwhelming, and she longed to be unconscious.

23

Summer felt as rotten as the lake water of dog days, as Margaret's mother called the post–Fourth of July swimming prospects. Teddy did not call, and Margaret worried what she would say if he did.

Soon after Margaret stopped mentioning Teddy to Grace and Isabelle, Grace began to badger her.

"I haven't asked you for five days," Grace said. Margaret had been spending time drawing or playing Monopoly with the twins. She made up excuses to avoid Grace. Sometimes she saw Grace's bike parked in front of Isabelle's house.

"Five days," she repeated, as they walked to the Dairy Queen on a ninety-two-degree day. "Something happened with Teddy. Why won't you tell us? How long can you hold it in?"

Little Teddy trotted ahead of them, turning to look back at the girls at each crosswalk.

"We just don't go out. That's it. It wasn't fun anymore," Margaret said, wishing that she hadn't agreed to go to the Dairy Queen.

"Grace," said Isabelle. "If she wants to tell us, she will, when she wants to."

"Just admit that it's not because it wasn't fun," Grace said. "Having known you forever, I will not accept that."

"Grace," said Isabelle, "She doesn't want to tell us. But if you stop harassing her, she might tell us in the future."

"You're repeating yourself," said Grace, blowing upward in an attempt to lift sweat-soaked bangs off her forehead. "She's gone dull on us, and she spends time with children, and she isn't any fun when we're together."

"It's because you won't let go of what *you* want to know."

"So there's nothing to talk about," said Grace. "I'm taking my DQ home, where at least there's life."

"Grace, you're being petulant," said Isabelle. "Our lives didn't revolve around Margaret and Teddy a few months ago."

"It's not a big deal," Margaret said. "I'll tell you sometime, just not now." When could she tell them? Grace saw Teddy at work. What if she told Grace and she inadvertently gave him a knowing look when he approached the pie counter? Even that would be a betrayal.

At home, Mark stopped asking questions after a few days. Mom told him that most people went out with a lot of different people before settling on one.

"Teddy got the wrong one out of the way pretty fast," he said. "At least I have his phone number." Margaret didn't hear that he had tried to call Teddy.

The twins stared at Margaret a lot and whispered to each other as they did so. Dad tried to be even heartier than usual.

With the lake looking like a cesspool at the beginning of August, the girls sat on the beach and contemplated the coming school year. Even Grace had dropped the subject of Teddy, although they continued to see each other at work.

"We didn't do as well as we thought we would with those three goals you had for us, Grace," Isabelle said, as she watched Little Teddy attempt to capture an abandoned beach ball, which rolled farther away with every touch of the puppy's paw.

"I still have a job," Grace said. "And a driver's permit. I'm glad I got rid of Lonnie. He was too expensive."

"Grace, I still can't believe that you paid his towing fee when he was the one who insisted on parking in a restricted zone," Isabelle said.

"I had to pay it. I told you that my purse was in the car when it was towed."

"Is he ever going to pay you back?" Margaret asked, happy for a shift to the travails of Grace.

"Of course," she said. "When he sells the car."

Margaret didn't repeat Grace's earlier claim that the car was worthless. She didn't have the energy to argue.

At the end of August, Teddy called Margaret.

"Would you have lunch with me sometime?" he asked.

They went to Bridgeman's the next day.

"I really want to tell Grace and Isabelle why we're not going out," Margaret said, before she ordered. "We're one unit, a lot of the time, and we share everything. The three of us will know, but no one else will."

"But you didn't tell Grace that you were going out with me at first, did you?" Teddy said. "You kept that to yourself for a while."

"I don't want to do that again, keep something about my personal life from my best friends."

Teddy ate a couple of bites of his cheeseburger. He didn't look at her.

"What are you thinking?" Margaret asked.

"I'm thinking that this is my life, not knowing who knows and who doesn't."

Margaret didn't know what to say that would make him feel better, because it was his life and he didn't think he could change it.

But Teddy looked so listless that she said, "Think of Little Teddy. If he bit someone—let's say, some nasty little kid in the alley who was poking him with a stick through the fence, and Little Teddy bloodied this kid's fingers—no one who loved the little guy would care that he was a biter. They wouldn't care what he'd done with his teeth, because they loved his big heart."

"Margaret, that's not a good analogy," said Teddy. "But I appreciate that you tried."

"I don't know what to do," Margaret said. "I feel like I lost my boyfriend and now I'm losing Grace. Isabelle has patience. Grace does not."

Teddy looked so sad that Margaret said, "It's not about me, is it? I'm sorry. It's really hard for you, I know. I mean, how can you have a boyfriend?"

"I can't. If I had a boyfriend, I couldn't go where anyone I know would see us. My life is a lie."

Margaret couldn't think of a response.

"I don't want to be this way," Teddy said.

Margaret waited.

"I want to be whatever 'normal' is."

Margaret couldn't imagine what she could say. A horrible thought appeared. What would her mother do? Here she was, too inexperienced to know how to save Teddy from despair. But her mother, the victim of a boring life, could think of the right words. After all, she knew that bad things happened, and she practiced saying appropriate things at all the funerals she went to when her ancient relatives and neighbors died off. This is the low point of my life, Margaret thought. I am channeling my mother, whose idea of a good time is to watch a detective show and share popcorn with Dad on Friday night—one of the three nights she didn't take out her mending basket.

"Teddy," she said, hoping that she didn't sound like a parent. "Someone you love will love you back. I know something good will happen." She didn't continue because she wasn't sure that she believed what she'd said.

Teddy stared as if he wanted to believe that she knew something he didn't know. Tears began to leak out of his eyes, and Margaret handed him her paper napkin because it seemed less greasy than his.

After Teddy had paid and they were on the sidewalk, Teddy growled as he grabbed Margaret's wrist and pretended to bite her hand.

"You Teddys are all alike," she said. "Biters at heart." It was a relief to be laughing so hard that she was crying as she tried to pull her hand away from Teddy's mouth.

She moved over to make room for the girls who were walking toward Bridgeman's.

"Hello, Margaret. Hello, Teddy," said Daisy Winter, as she and her friends passed. "Get a leash."

Margaret and Teddy sat on the curb until they had stopped laughing, which took a long time because when either of them caught their breath, the other one said, "Get a leash."

The car ride home felt relaxed, and Margaret didn't feel the need to talk or revisit what had already been said.

Teddy turned the car off when they reached Margaret's house. "Do you want me to come in and say hi to your mom and the kids?" he asked.

"They would really like that."

"Okay. Here we go." Teddy didn't open the car door to exit. "Margaret," he said. "You can tell Isabelle and Grace if you have to." He sounded resigned.

Margaret looked at the side of Teddy's face until he turned to look at her.

"Thank you," she said.

24

Sitting on the almost deserted main beach at Lake Harriet near the end of August, Margaret told Grace and Isabelle that she was going to tell them something about Teddy.

"You have to promise that you won't tell anyone, ever," she said. "If you can't do that, it's okay. I don't have to tell you if you don't think it's possible to promise."

Grace put her right hand over her heart and her left arm up, bent at the elbow.

"I promise to God that any secret will be safe with me until I die, including but not limited to time spent under sedation and time talking in my sleep."

"I need more than that, Grace," said Margaret.

"Does anyone do 'drawn-and-quartered' anymore? I promise to volunteer for that but I won't need to because I'm loyal."

"What else?"

"I have an excellent record. I never told anyone that you 'filled your pants' in second grade. I mean, I never told anyone who didn't already know. I never told anyone that you and Sherman had a plan to hide out together until his family had relocated."

"I do trust you, Grace." She turned to Isabelle. "You would never tell anyone what I'm going to tell you, would you?"

"I promise that I won't."

"Okay."

"We've known each other since we were embryos," said Grace. "Why does Isabelle get off so lightly?"

"Because she's Isabelle."

Margaret knew that neither Grace nor Isabelle would break a promise. One of the reasons was that the three of them had each other with whom to dissect endless minutiae; they didn't need to break and re-create alliances, because they had each other to talk every situation to death.

After she told them about the night at the lake and what Teddy had told her, Grace said, "I think I'm going to be sick."

"Grace, do you remember when the three of us were on my porch in the summer and we all finally knew about sex?" Margaret asked.

"How could I forget? We were in collective shock, and Isabelle said, 'If your mom can do it, Margaret, I guess we can do it if we have to.'"

"So, I guess people must want to do it with somebody sometime," Margaret said.

"I don't like to think about it," said Isabelle. "Do you think that you'll keep seeing Teddy?"

"I don't know," Margaret said. "It's kind of sad to think of being with him and kind of sad to think of never seeing him. I don't know what he wants either. It hurts to think about it, how he pretends."

"Are your parents in mourning?" asked Isabelle.

"They're okay. My mom doesn't have to worry about what I might do on a blanket with Teddy. No more late nights for her."

"Do you think he used you? You know, like a cover?" Isabelle asked.

Did she want to admit this? "I do," she said. "He did. But I can't hate him, because it just seems sad, really sad."

"You never know what's around the corner," said Grace. "It's a mystery. How Teddy looks like someone on the cover of a Harlequin romance but isn't what he seems."

"How Little Teddy is swimming out to the dock," said Isabelle.

The lifeguard was blowing his whistle in the direction of Little Teddy.

"What does that lifeguard think, that Teddy will turn around to find what's piercing his puppy eardrums?" Grace asked.

"He's never gone in the water before," said Isabelle, as she stood up.

"This proves something," said Grace, as she and Margaret began to run after Isabelle, who was racing after Little Teddy. "We don't know anything. About anybody. About anything, even our dog."

"No, Grace," said Margaret, as she sailed over a sandcastle. "We know a lot of things. It's just that every time we figure something out, there's something that we never thought of, coming right at us."

Margaret stayed even with Grace, although Grace usually outran her. There was relief in knowing that they—and maybe the lifeguard, in a boat—could save someone, even if it was a crazy little dog that didn't know what he was doing or where he was headed.

Grace and Margaret caught up with Isabelle, who grabbed Margaret's hand, and Margaret extended her hand to Grace. Little Teddy was already swimming back from the ropes that cordoned off the shallow water from the deep.

ACKNOWLEDGMENTS

Loretta Ellsworth, Janet Graber, Phyllis Root, and Nolan Zavoral—wonderful writers all—have my deep gratitude for the many hours that they listened to *Whatever Normal Is* and encouraged me. Many thanks to Anders Hanson and Mighty Media; the characters Margaret, Grace, and Isabelle are honored to have their stories so whimsically, artfully, and knowingly presented. Erik Anderson and the delightful and dedicated staff of the University of Minnesota Press have given the girls a chance to be heard, for which I am forever grateful.

Jane St. Anthony grew up in south Minneapolis in a house with a front porch that was perfect for summer reading. She is a freelance writer and leads workshops for young authors at writing and education conferences. She has written three other books for middle-grade readers: *The Summer Sherman Loved Me*, *Grace Above All*, and *Isabelle Day Refuses to Die of a Broken Heart*, all published by the University of Minnesota Press. She lives in Minneapolis.